Felicia C. Gaines

Savannah in Waiting

Savannah in Waiting
An Independent Publication

First North American Publication 2013

Cover Design © Karen L. Syed

Technical Production Consultant:
Karen L. Syed at Sassy Gal Enterprises

Felicia Gaines
Claire's Creative Corner
fcgainesauthor@gmail.com

ISBN 13: 978-0615885452
ISBN: 0-615-88545-4

This book is dedicated to my mother, who is currently battling stage-four cancer. Mom, you are the strongest person I know and I would not be the person I am today if it weren't for you. You will always have my love and my heart.

I would like to acknowledge my sister T.B. who has been a major help through this whole process; love you, sis. Thank you also to my friends and family for all their encouragement; you guys are the best and you know who you are.

Thank you to my husband for just being there to listen when I need you; I love you dearly.

One

The sign outside the little coffee house read, *La Maison Du Cafe*. Savannah Monreaux was experiencing France for the first time. Having arrived that day, she couldn't wait to get out and enjoy the sites.

She'd made the decision to travel to France some time ago, so she barely believed she was actually sitting in a French coffeehouse.

So many factors had led her to this time and place she could hardly take it all in. Savannah thought at this stage in her life she would have had a family, or at least be married.

The cafe looked adorable with its white linen tablecloths covering each round table. They offered intimate seating for two or tables of four for conversations with friends.

Savannah walked up to the counter and waited her

turn in line.

"What can I get you?" the young man at the counter asked with a friendly smile.

"One coffee, please." Savannah smiled back.

"Please have a seat and someone will bring it right out." She found a table in the corner away from any movement, and sat with her back against the wall peering about.

Minutes later, she heard a voice. "Here you are, Madame." He held a dainty china cup filled with aromatic brew on a beautiful decorative plate.

Reaching for the cup, Savannah asked where she might find creamer. While the server explained the service center to the left, a smile came across her face, bringing to mind her father. She remembered how he used to tease her about the way she drank her coffee. He called it *coffee milk* because she'd put so much creamer in it, but that's the way she liked it, not too strong, and exceptionally sweet. Taking her first sip she closed her eyes, savoring the taste and smell. When she opened her eyes, she watched the most handsome man she'd ever seen enter the room. He stood well over six feet tall with broad shoulders complementing his muscular physique. His dark curly locks with hints of red and brown looked as if someone had placed each one there by hand. His eyes smoldered a remarkable shade of green. He walked with the authority of a man who might own the place. Savannah felt the air being sucked from her lungs as she watched him intently.

"May I help you?" The young man who had served Savannah minutes earlier waited for the newcomer's response.

"One dark roast coffee, please," he said, his voice stern.

"Please have a seat; someone will bring that right out."

The man took a seat in the center of the cafe, and began reading a newspaper. Savannah stared at the man while trying not to be noticed. How dignified and refined; his presence commanded the attention of everyone in the room. After some time, he put his paper down, finished his coffee, and left without even glancing around the cafe. Disappointed he hadn't noticed her, Savannah thought; a man of such stature would never be interested in an unsophisticated girl like her. After spending most of the day shopping and sightseeing, Savannah retreated back to her chateau for a long hot bath before heading to bed.

She lay staring at small imperfections in the ceiling while remembering the man she'd seen in the cafe that morning. Her mind drifted as images of her past life came flooding in. She was thirty-nine years old and would turn forty while in France. She'd given herself this gift for her birthday. She'd promised she'd make it to Paris before her fortieth birthday, and she had. But what of all the years before now she wondered, were they wasted?

What could I have done differently? How could I have given more meaning to my life? For the first time, she faced the question, who is Savannah, and where is she headed? Ever since her childhood friends had teased her for being the good little girl; never smoking or drinking, and always doing what she'd been told, and what everyone expected of her. However, Savannah had become desperate for change from what had become her oh so ordinary life. She rolled over, thinking again of the man from the coffee shop. He'd looked so delicious, surely he must be married, or at least attached. Snap out of it, she thought, when suddenly a pair of striking green eyes took over, and she fell asleep.

* * *

Morning came, bright and beautiful. She decided to go to the coffee house for breakfast, hoping to see the same pair of green eyes. Savannah arrived at the cafe around the same time as the day before, ordered a coffee, and sat at the same table facing the door. By noon, the stranger hadn't come, and Savannah began to realize just how foolish she'd been for wasting her time. Leaving the café, she decided to do more shopping. She still had gifts to buy.

Savannah stepped off the curb just as a limo pulled out in front of her. The door opened, and a chauffeur stepped to open the door for his passenger.

Out stepped a man, but not just any man. Magnificent green eyes, just as she remembered from the coffee house, looked back at her.

"Excuse me, I didn't mean to block your way," he said.

"What?" Savannah found it hard to utter a word.

"I'm sorry. I didn't mean to block your way."

"Oh, it's all right," she said.

Smiling down at her, he hesitated a moment, staring into her eyes. Suddenly, he stepped aside and walked away.

Go on, she thought, say something, and ask him his name. By the time Savannah regained her ability to communicate, he'd already gone.

The long black limo sped away. As Savannah watched she saw the license plate, it read Mansfield. During lunch, she pondered ways to find out more about her mystery man. She had only one clue to go on, the name Mansfield. *What am I doing?* She'd never done anything like this. She knew nothing of this man other than how handsome and so far out of her league he seemed.

Most people considered Savannah, a girl from the deep South–a smorgasbord of nationalities consisting of African American, French, Spanish, and Native American referred to as Creole in her native bayou land–beautiful, though she didn't think so. Those same people said her light brown eyes told a story when you looked in them. Olive-colored skin showed no visible flaws, and long thick unruly hair spent most days pulled up in a ponytail. Savannah had a normal childhood, except for the times being teased by the other kids for not fitting into one nationality. She'd never felt White or Black, and to look at her, no one else could tell either. Savannah's friends chastised her style of dress as leaving something to be desired. She wore baggy plaid shirts, and blue jeans with worn out tennis shoes every day, unless working. Her hair lacked the luster of time and patience, and was not something she focused on. She didn't come from money; her family worked regular jobs, which kept a roof over their heads. They did well. Though she'd graduated from college with an accounting degree, she'd made no extraordinary strides in her life.

After getting herself a bite to eat, she wandered back to the chateau and got on the Internet. To her surprise, there were only two entries with the name Mansfield in France; one being Mansfield Enterprises, a multi-billion dollar corporation built up by oil field investments and the buying out of companies who were unable to carry on due to financial strain. She printed out the map, and address to the corporate office then decided to get some sleep. The next morning she headed off to 2413 Winchester Avenue; the corporate office of Mansfield Enterprises. She had no idea what she would do or say when she got there, but felt compelled to continue. She pulled up to a building taller than any she'd seen in her life; she found a parking spot, and sat there for what felt like hours.

You can do this, she said to herself, stepping out of her rental car. As she entered the building, she noticed the décor, breathtaking with its textured walls, beautiful tiled floors, and exquisite artwork. Savannah walked to the receptionist's desk.

"Is Mr. Mansfield available?"

"Do you have an appointment, *mademoiselle*?" asked the receptionist.

Stunned by what she'd just done, Savannah stammered, "No. No, I don't."

"Mr. Mansfield is available by appointment only. Would you like to schedule one? What business do you represent?"

"Represent?" Savannah flushed. *What on earth am I doing*? Pursuing a man in such a way? She turned around and quickly walked out of the building and right into the arms of her handsome stranger, spilling his coffee, and newspaper onto the lobby floor. Savannah, trembling, began picking up the papers while apologizing, her face burning. Without Looking up, Savannah handed him his papers.

"Thank you," he said in a deep soft voice. Raising her head to look at him, she stared into his wondrous eyes.

"Oh my goodness, it's you?"

11

"I'm so sorry, Mr. Mansfield, truly I am."

"Excuse me? Do I know you? Haven't I seen you before?"

"Savannah, my, my name is Savannah Monreaux."

"Well, Ms. Monreaux, the accident was my fault; I'm hurrying to a meeting."

He stared at her, thinking what beautiful skin she had, as if kissed by the sun.

Upon noticing her clothes, he couldn't help but wonder what brought her to his building? Feeling a little confused, Larson watched as her figure vanished out the glass door.

Before heading up to the office, Larson stopped at the receptionist desk for messages.

"Good morning, Elise, are there any messages for me?"

"No, sir, but the woman who just ran you over inquired about you."

"Really," he said. "What did she want?"

"She didn't say, sir."

Larson wondered what she could want with him. Savannah... He was sure he'd seen her before.

Savannah returned to the chateau, embarrassed. She pulled up the Internet and decided to do more research on Mansfield enterprises. Larson Mansfield, a prominent figure in France had been born into wealth. His mother, the elegant and sophisticated Caroline, inherited millions after her parents died in a plane crash. Larson's father had also been born into privilege, with what some called old money, which had been passed down through generations, and left to his only living heir, Larson.

Not only were the Mansfield's rich, but according to the gossip, they had no idea how the rest of the world lived. Larson had reached forty and remained unmarried; not for lack of trying on his part.

Rumors abounded that Caroline, his mother, kept a firm hand on the woman he dated. From what Savannah read, hardworking Larson was nothing like his mother; his life didn't revolve around his families' worth. He showed compassion for life, and people, something his mother made clear she considered a fault.

Work for Larson the rest of the day remained busy, with Caroline counting on him for everything, but he didn't mind; he loved the rush and thrill of his job, much like his father.

* * *

The next day on his way to the office, Larson once again found himself thinking about the woman from the day before. *Savannah.* Larson stopped at the coffee house for his usual cup before heading to work. They made the best coffee in town and stopping there before work had become part of his daily ritual. Walking in, he noticed a familiar face in the corner. He walked over to her, "Hi, Savannah, right?"

Savannah mumbled softly, "Larson, right?"

"May I join you?"

"Certainly." Remembering the day before, she began to apologize for practically running him over.

"You seemed to be in quite a bit of a hurry," said Larson.

"Now that you mentioned it, what *were* you doing at my office?"

Savannah simply stared into his beautiful eyes as her heart skipped a beat.

"My secretary said you wanted to see me. Have we met before?"

He waited.

"Ms. Monreaux?"

"I'm sorry did you say something?" asked Savannah.

"I asked what you were doing at my office."

"Okay, don't think I'm a stalker, but this isn't the first time I've seen you at this coffee house. I also saw you on the street."

She stammered on.

"Now that I've totally embarrassed myself, I'd better go."

"No wait." His hand gently touched her elbow. "I'd like to get to know you better; if that's okay. I have a meeting this morning, and have to leave. I'll leave you my number, and let you decide if you want to use it."

14

Desperately wanting to get to know him, she reached out and took the card, touching his fingertips in the process. Savannah blushed as she smiled, slowly moving her hand back.

Larson smiled as he stood, saying, "I hope to hear from you soon."

Savannah sat wondering if her mind were playing tricks on her. Had that just happened?

Had the most handsome man she'd ever met spoken to her? She got up from the table and stood watching as he drove off.

Finally, she'd met her mystery man. Should she call or was he just being polite.

* * *

A few days went by, and she hadn't called Larson. Savannah had become restless, and knew her time in France soon would be coming to an end. She had taken only three weeks off from work and was well into her first week. She left the chateau and decided to do some sightseeing. There was a small gift shop where she went for souvenirs, she still needed gifts to take back home for her parents, and friends. Savannah's day had been fantastic. She had fallen in love with France and would regret having to leave. Upon returning to the chateau, Savannah checked for messages at the front desk. Wishing Larson had called, but realized she hadn't given him her number. With a giggle, she reached into her pocket and found his number folded up on a piece of paper. How silly she felt, all this time having his number and waiting for him to call when he had no way to contact her. Once in the room, she opened the piece of paper with shaking hands. What do I do? She wondered. She'd waited days to talk to him, and now for no reason she was unsure. She slowly picked up the phone and dialed the number.

"Mansfield residence; Charles speaking. How may I help you?"

Savannah's heart felt as though it was in her throat. Finally, mustering up the courage to speak, she said, "Mr. Larson Mansfield, please."

"May I say who is calling?"

"Yes, this is Ms. Savannah Monreaux."

"One moment please."

Savannah listened as she waited.

"Mr. Mansfield, I have Ms. Savannah Monreaux on the line, sir."

"Thank you, Charles, I'll take it in the study."

Savannah thought about hanging up, but before she could a voice on the phone said, "Larson Mansfield speaking."

"Mr. Mansfield, its Savannah Monreaux." Savannah tried to calm herself on the phone, but her insides tossed and tumbled as though she'd been on a carnival ride.

"I'm surprised you called! I didn't think you would," Larson said enthusiastically.

"I wasn't sure I would either," she whispered.

"I'm hoping you will agree to have dinner with me tomorrow."

"Why, Mr. Mansfield, I hardly know you."

"Well, it would give the two of us a chance to change all that, don't you think, Ms. Monreaux? After all, it is only dinner."

Savannah took a deep breath and agreed.

"Great," said Larson. "I'll call you with the details."

"I'm looking forward to it."

When Savannah got off the phone, she began to panic. She had nothing fit to wear for such an occasion, and beat up old jeans, with a plaid shirt just wouldn't do.

What in the world was she going to do with her hair and what about makeup? She wasn't accustomed to dinners at fancy restaurants. If she were at home, she'd be eating crawfish with her hands.

Savannah decided she needed help. She would make an appointment to get her hair done, but being so overwhelmed left her out of her element. She continued to panic, Justine; she'll know what to do. If a best friend couldn't manage to calm my anxiety, no one could. Dialing the number, her fingers trembled.

"Justine."

"Savannah, is that you?"

"What's wrong?"

"Are you all right?"

"I'm fine, Justine, everything is fine." She sucked in a deep breath.

"I need to talk with you. I met a man who's asked me out to dinner, and I have no idea how to get myself together.

"Savannah, I'm surprised at you; just be yourself and everything will be fine."

"You don't understand, Justine; he owns one of the most successful companies in the world. He's rich, sophisticated, and so handsome."

"Savannah, your mother and father raised you to have pride in yourself, no matter how much or how little you had. Just be Savannah." Justine paused.

"That said, what do you know about this man, other than the obvious?"

"Well, he seems very nice."

"Savannah, you don't know much about this man."

"Are you sure you want to go on this dinner date?"

"I'd like to get to know him better, and a conversation over dinner would help."

"Speaking of dinner what are you going to wear? And please tell me you're doing something with that ponytail."

"That's why I called; I need your sense of style," Savannah said, laughing until all seemed serious again.

"Savannah just be yourself. If he can accept you as you are then he likes you for you if not then maybe he's not the one. I know you, Savannah; you're a jeans and T-shirt kind of girl with little or no makeup. Let him get to know the real you. Unless this is a fancy dinner let him see the real you."

Justine, I know you're worried, but I'll be okay."

"Fine, Savannah, but you call me as soon as you get in."

"I promise, don't worry."

* * *

Savannah woke the next day as nervous as she'd gone to sleep. Larson had called as promised, with the details that the limo would pick her up at 8:00 p.m.

Taking her best friends advice, she pulled her hair back, put on a blouse, a pair of slacks, and a little lip gloss. She stared at herself in the mirror for a few minutes.

"Oh well, this will have to do I suppose."

Two

It was 7:30 p.m., Savannah wondered what their conversation would be like, and would he notice how nervous she was. Suddenly, the doorbell rang, out front sat a long black limo to pick her up.

"Hello, Ms. Monreaux, I'm Charles, Mr. Mansfield's chauffeur. I'm here to take you to the restaurant."

Savannah took one last deep breath and headed out the door.

On the way to the restaurant, she kept thinking about Justine's words. *Just be yourself, Savannah.*

They arrived at the restaurant, and Charles opened the door for her to step out of the limo. She barely felt her legs beneath her. She took a moment to compose herself, and stepped onto the glamorous red carpet lining the entrance to the doorway. Suddenly, she felt terribly underdressed.

"May I help you?"

"Reservations for Mansfield," she said.

"Right this way please," said the host behind the podium.

As Savannah drew near the table, she saw Larson sitting there. He looked even more attractive than she remembered. When she approached the table, he stood, eyes wide open.

"Hello, Savannah, I'm so glad you decided to join me."

As he pulled out her chair, she faded, for a moment, back to the coffee house, and the first time she'd seen him.

"So, Savannah, how are you enjoying your visit? Is Paris everything you wished it would be?"

She wanted to shout out that because of him, her wish had come true, but instead said, "I've been enjoying the sights. It's truly beautiful here."

After some small talk, they decided to order.

"I'm really not sure what to get."

"I'm sorry," said Larson. "Are you having trouble with the menu? I can translate it to you if you like."

Savannah laughed softly.

"No, thank you; I speak and read French. Well, Cajun French anyway, but I can figure it out." After they laughed a little, she said, "But maybe you could tell me what would be a good choice. I'm assuming this isn't your first time here?"

After ordering dinner, they continued with the small talk. Savannah became so nervous her stomach was in knots.

"Savannah, tell me about your family?"

She thought for a moment and said, "I guess we're your typical everyday family. I grew up in a middle class home. My dad worked the shipyard, and my mom worked as a schoolteacher until they both retired a few years ago. They met in high school and married soon after graduation."

For some reason, she wished she'd said something else. She didn't know why, but she felt ashamed for even thinking it.

"I'm sorry," she said. "I wish my family was a little more interesting, but it is what it is."

"Don't be sorry, I think it's sweet. So how long have they been married?"

"It will be forty-seven years this year."

As he raised his head and looked into her eyes, he whispered, "They must truly love each other."

Larson's mother and father had been married for many years before his father died, but he always wondered whether they ever genuinely loved each other. He hoped they had, but that seemed so long ago.

"Larson, are you okay?"

"Yes," he said, while thinking of his mother and father.

"What about your family? What are they like?"

Savannah asked.

"Well, my dad was a very caring man, but firm. He put so much time into his work, I hardly ever saw him. My mom, on the other hand, can take some time getting used to. She's the kind of woman who takes pride in knowing she has control of everyone's life."

"She can't be that awful," said Savannah.

"Well, you tell me what you think when you meet her."

"Meet her? What do you mean?"

"I'd like you to have dinner with us this week; I'd like the two of you to meet."

Savannah know for certain wasn't ready for that.

However, when she opened her mouth all that came out was, "Sure I'd love to."

"Great, then I'll set everything up and call you."

Larson drove Savannah home and walked her to the door. Before leaving, he reached over and kissed her ever so gently on the cheek.

"Goodnight, Savannah I had a wonderful time, and look forward to seeing you again soon."

As soon as she had gotten in the doorway, she called Justine so she wouldn't worry.

"Justine."

"Savannah, is that you?"

"Hi, Justine, I made it back to the chateau."

"Oh great, did you have a good time?"

"The best," said Savannah, "but let me fill you in

23

tomorrow I want to try and get some sleep."

Getting any sleep would prove to be a challenge for Savannah; her mind kept replaying that night, and how incredible it was.

* * *

The next morning when she woke, she wondered if it had all been a dream until the phone rang, with Larson on the other end.

"Good morning Savannah, I hope I didn't wake you."

"Not at all." She had hardly slept a wink.

I wanted to see if you were available tomorrow night for dinner with my mother.

"Tomorrow night? Dinner with your mother?" she asked in a nervous tone.

"Yes," he replied, "is that all right with you?"

She thought for a moment and then said, "Yes."

"I will send the limo to pick you up say, around 7:00 p.m."

"That would be great," said Savannah, "seven it is."

That whole day she worried and paced the floor wondering what she was going to wear and what his mother might be like. Looking through her clothes she decided to get something new to wear, and with that a makeover, as well. She decided to go into the city and see what was available; she knew she needed help if she were to impress his mother.

24

Savannah decided to let go, and get a complete makeover. She went down to the lobby and asked the front-desk clerk if there were any salons near bye where she could get a whole new look.

"There's a fantastic salon just two blocks from here; ask for Robar. Tell him Juliet sent you."

* * *

Savannah arrived at the salon and went inside.

"Hi, may I help you?"

"Yes, I'm looking for Robar."

"I am Robar; Juliet called and said you needed my help. Let me see what I'll be working with."

Savannah took down her hair; it was long and unruly, but thick, and beautiful.

"So, Ms. Monreaux, are you ready for a change?"

"I think so, what exactly do you have in mind?" Just lay your head back and try not to worry, you're in good hands.

After an hour and a half, Robar finished, but would not let Savannah turn around until Angele worked on her makeup.

"Are you ready to see the new you?" asked Robar?

As the chair began to spin around, she could feel her heart pounding in her throat. Who is this woman in the mirror? She's too beautiful to be me, but she had my face. Her hair was straight and silky smooth with highlights of red. Her hair had been layered around her face as though it were hugging it. Her makeup looked soft, yet subtle, but with warm tones. She couldn't believe the reflection staring back at her. She appeared different but in a good way. She still needed to get dressed, as it was getting late. Larson would be there soon with the limo to pick her up.

"Okay, honey," said Robar. "Elise is waiting for you in the dressing room with some dresses. She will finish up this fabulous transformation for you." Savannah was not accustomed to wearing dresses and heels, she had always worn flats. She didn't even know if she could wear heals. After trying on a few dresses, she walked out in front of the mirror.

It was the most exquisite shade of blue she had ever seen. It hugged her body like a glove; showing a portion of her body she didn't know existed. She was ready and excited about meeting Larson's mother. It would be an exciting night she thought.

* * *

Back at the mansion things were not pleasant.

"Why do I have to meet her, can't you just wait for a month or two for her to go away like all the rest of the woman you've dated?"

"Mother, I really like Savannah, so please promise you'll be on your best behavior."

"I'll try, but no promises. Who names their child after a city anyway?"

"Mother, please. You promised."

"I said I'd try; beyond that I have no control."

The limo arrived at seven sharp, and when Savannah stepped out onto the curb, she was stunning. Using her cell phone she called her mother to let her know she would be out and not have her phone on just in case she tried to call.

"Hi, Mom, well I'm on my way so wish me luck."

"You don't need it, dear; they're going to love you."

"Thanks, Mom, I'll call you in the morning."

"Call me when you get in, Savannah, no matter what time it is."

Arriving at the mansion, Savannah began to have second thoughts and considered going back to the chateau. Just then a little voice inside said, now we didn't come this far to turn around did we. She stepped out of the car and was escorted to the door. She walked in and waited for a bit when she heard Larson's voice.

"Savannah is that you?" She was beautiful he thought, even more beautiful than he'd remembered. He took her shawl but couldn't speak. After a few moments of awkward silence, he said. "I'm so glad you're here, everyone is in the dining room shall we join them."

"Larson, did you just say everyone? I thought it would be only the three of us."

"Me as well, but when I told mother I wanted her to meet you, she invited a few of her colleagues to join us."

When they entered the dining room, everyone went quiet. Savannah could feel her palms starting to sweat as Larson spoke.

"Attention everyone, I'd like you to meet my date, Ms. Savannah Monreaux. Savannah this is..." He introduced her to everyone at the table until finally she stood in front of his mother.

"Mother, this is Ms. Savannah Monreaux. Savannah, this is my mother, Ms. Caroline Mansfield."

Savannah reached out her hand, "So nice to meet you."

After what seemed like forever, Caroline loosely grasped Savannah's hand. "I've heard a great deal about you, Ms. Monreaux."

Savannah felt a sudden chill in the air. It's just nerves she thought.

"Ms. Monreaux, sit next to me please, I'd like to get to know you better," said Caroline.

The evening went slowly, and Savannah couldn't help but notice that Caroline barely said a word to her all night.

Larson, on the other hand, had been wonderful the entire night. He was so refined, and when he looked at her his green eyes seem to pierce right through her. The dinner party was full of executives, big shots trying to figure out how to get more money out of their businesses.

"Attention everyone, I'd like to make a toast,"

boasted Caroline. "Thanks to good friends, co-workers and business partners, Also, I'd like to thank my son for introducing us all to his new friend Sylvia."

"It's Savannah," said a small almost fragile voice.

"I'm sorry, did I say that wrong?" Caroline smirked.

Larson gave his mother a disapproving look from behind Savannah as she continued her toast.

Savannah waited until dinner ended before asking Larson to get her wrap.

"I'd like to go home please."

"Sure, Savannah, I'll take you home myself."

She stood, and said goodnight as Larson led her out of the dining room. He reached for her shawl, wrapped it around her shoulders, and opened the front door.

It was quiet in the car, neither said a word. Finally, Larson said, "I'm so sorry about tonight; my mother can sometimes be a handful."

Savannah took a deep breath. "I don't think she cares too much for me."

"It's not you. She has an issue with anyone I bring home."

"I wish you'd warned me in advance about your mother."

"Honestly, I thought if I told you…you wouldn't come."

Savannah sighed. "You're probably right."

"Enough talk about mother," he said. "I had a wonderful evening, and you look stunning."

The car pulled in front of the chateaux. Larson stepped out and opened Savannah the door. "May I see you again, Savannah?"

"I'd like that."

Larson looked at her and confessed, "I wish this night didn't have to end."

Savannah's lips curled up, forcing her to smile. Larson moved closer, and kissed her softly on her cheek; so close to her ear that she could feel the warmth of his breath against her skin.

"Good night, Savannah."

The beating of Savannah's heart had to stop pounding before she could manage a whisper.

"Good night, Larson."

The first thing she did was call her mother, she had promised to call as soon as she got in, no matter what time it was.

"Hi, Mom, we're you asleep?"

"That's okay, honey. How did your night go?"

She wasn't quite sure what parts to tell her. She didn't want to upset her, so she omitted the way Larson's mother ignored her, introducing her as Sylvia. Instead, she told her mother how wonderful Larson treated her, how he made her feel special.

"You are special, Savannah, always have been, never forget that," said Adele.

"Thanks, Mom. I'll call you tomorrow."

She was still thinking about Larson's kiss her on the cheek. It made her heart flutter again. She got a shower and headed off to bed she would be doing some sightseeing in the morning and wanted to be fully rested. But sleep did not come easy.

* * *

When the alarm went off at 7:00 a.m., she covered her head, wanting a few more minutes of sleep. Realizing she'd come fully awake, she pushed out of bed to get ready for the day ahead. Just, as, she headed out the door the phone began to ring. Trying to decide whether or not to get the phone, she came back in and answered it, on the other end she heard Larson's voice.

"Hi, Savannah, it's Larson, did I wake you?"

"No. No, you didn't, I'm just heading out to do some shopping and sightseeing."

"I was hoping we could have lunch together, would that be okay?"

"Yes," she said excitedly. Larson asked her what she would like to eat.

"Honestly, what I'd really like is comfort food, like pizza."

"Then pizza it is, I will send the limo for you."

Savannah said she'd take a cab and for Larson to point her in the right direction.

"Are you sure?"

"Yes, I'll meet you at the restaurant about noon.

The morning couldn't go by fast enough. When Savannah arrived he stood waiting for her at the front door. He looked so handsome, what could he possibly want with an ordinary country girl like me, thought Savannah. I have nothing to offer that could make a change in his life for the better.

"Savannah, it's so good to see you again."

"Good afternoon, Mr. Mansfield, table for two today."

"Yes, please, somewhere with a little privacy if you don't mind."

"Right this way, sir, I have just the spot."

They sat talking and laughing for hours. Neither one realized how late it had gotten. When Larson saw the time, he huffed in frustration and immediately called for the waitress.

"Check, please. Savannah, I'm so sorry I have to rush off this way, but I would like to make it up to you tonight if it's all right."

Looking into his eyes, she couldn't possibly say no.

"Can I call you later with details for dinner?"

"Dinner?" she asked. "I thought we just had dinner.

Larson laughed. "I thought that was lunch."

"Where I'm from," said Savannah, "noon is dinner."

"So, what are we having tonight?" Larson asked,

curiously."

"Why, supper of course," said Savannah.

"Then I'll be looking forward to supper."

He walked Savannah to the cab, opened her door, and said, "Until tonight."

As he leaned forward, she felt her pulse racing. The softness of his lips touched her cheek with such tenderness that she wasn't sure he had even kissed her goodbye. She watched him walk away; admiring the sway of his body, as though there were music playing only he could hear.

She sat for a minute trying to clear her head; she was still feeling weak from his touch as he motioned the cab driver on and faded in the distance. She went back to the chateau, there was no need to try and do anything else today. Her mind would be preoccupied thinking about tonight.

* * *

Larson walked into the board meeting which was already in session.

"Excuse me for interrupting, please, continue." During the board meeting, Larson could feel the stare of his mother piercing through his skin. After the meeting, he heard his mother's voice.

"Larson, would you stay seated please, we need to talk."

"Where were you?" asked Caroline.

"At lunch, Mother," he answered quickly.

"So you were with a client?"

Larson's silence made Caroline angry.

"Should I even ask who?"

"Ask only if you really want to know, Mother. I need you to stay out of my private life okay."

"I'm your mother; you have no private life as far as I'm concerned."

"I'm having dinner with Savannah tonight, Mother, so I won't be home to dine with you."

"What are you thinking, Larson? This girl is not of your stature. She doesn't fit into our world, and she will only get hurt in the process."

Larson left the room, but his mother's words lingered on his mind all day. He knew his mother, and she had a way of making the woman in his life miserable.

"Maybe I should call and cancel he thought to himself, but how can I do that feeling as I do about her."

Larson had finally begun to admit to himself that there was something about Savannah he had fallen for. And why not, she's beautiful, sensitive, and intelligent. There was a part of him that envied her. She was more in control of whom she was then he'd ever been. His life had been built on what people wanted and expected of him, especially his mother. He had to see her tonight, He longed for her conversation, longed to see her face and sun kissed skin. She was sweet and innocent of no fault of her own, maybe his mother was right. Maybe she didn't belong in his world. Larson picked up the phone and began to dial Savannah's number.

"Hello."

"Hi, Savannah, it's Larson, did I interrupt anything?"

"No, I'm just reading, and I guess I fell asleep."

As he listened to her voice on the other end of the phone, he contemplated breaking their engagement until Savannah said, "So where are we going tonight?"

"How about this wonderful Italian restaurant, I know. Do you like Italian food?"

"Wonderful, I love Italian food as evident from lunch," she said, laughing."

"I'll be there to pick you up at 8:00 p.m."

Savannah leaped up, trying to find something to wear, but nothing seemed right. She remembered seeing boutiques downstairs just past the lobby; maybe she could find something to wear for her special evening.

She jumped into the shower; the hot water loosened the muscles of her taut nerves. Looking at the clock, she realized time was moving faster than her. She slipped on some shorts and a T-shirt and headed for the boutique. She walked into the shop and smiled when the sales clerk greeted her. "Hello, I'm Sasha. Are you looking for anything in particular?"

"Hi, I'm Savannah; I'm going to dinner tonight and really need something to wear."

"Is this a special dinner or just a night out with friends?"

Savannah lowered her lashes.

"Oh," said Sasha. "This is someone special."

Savannah blushed.

"I have just the thing," she said. A few moments later she brought Savannah a fiery red dress to try on.

"A dress?" Savannah frowned.

"Yes, this is perfect for your body. Go ahead, try it on."

Too nervous to come out, Savannah lingered in the dressing room for some time.

"Savannah, are you okay in there?" questioned Sasha.

"Fine, but I'm not sure about this dress, I think it needs more material."

"Come on out and let me take a look."

Savannah stepped out of the dressing room.

"So what do you think?"

"Oh my, you look sensational." Sasha covered her open mouth.

"Really, you think so?"

"Yes, this is perfect for your date; he must be quite remarkable."

Savannah thought for a moment as she smiled again; it seemed that happened a lot lately at the mention of Larson.

"Miss, Savannah, if I may make a suggestion; I have just the right shoes for this dress."

Savannah rubbed one foot across the top of the other nervously. She wasn't used to wearing heals and hoped it wasn't what Sasha had in mind.

"These will be great not too high, I promise."

Savannah slipped her feet into the shoes. "They're perfect."

"You look stunning."

"Thank you so much, I couldn't have done this without your help." Savannah paid at the register, gathered her things, and went back to the chateau to get ready.

Moments after she put on her final touches, the phone rang. Charles let her know he had arrived to pick her up. She grabbed her handbag and keys and hurried out the door. Charles stood by the car smiling.

"Good evening, Ms. Monreaux, forgive me for staring, but I nearly didn't recognize you."

"I hope that's a good thing."

"Most certainly," said Charles.

They arrived at the restaurant on time, and Larson sat at the table waiting. Savannah's palms started to sweat as she thought about retreating.

"This way, Ms. Monreaux," said the waiter.

Suddenly, she stood face to face with Larson. It seemed as if time stopped until she heard Larson say,

"Oh, wow."

He stood and pulled out Savannah's chair. 'Her cheeks heated as she noticed him staring.

"Savannah, you are absolutely breathtaking."

"Thank you," she said as her face burned with an oddly pleasant embarrassment.

Several times during dinner, Larson lost track of the conversation and stumbled over his words.

"Larson, are you all right? You seem a bit pre-occupied."

"I'm sorry the truth is I'm having trouble concentrating with you next to me."

She lowered her lashes.

"Did I embarrass you?" Larson asked.

"A little, but don't stop."

Dinner tasted superb and the atmosphere euphoric. Savannah warmed as Larson took her hand in his and asked her to dance. As she stood, he placed his other hand on the small of her back and led her to the dance floor. When she stepped into his arms, she could barely breathe while taking in the essence of his cologne. Dancing, she feared her legs might give way as he pulled her closer.

"I'm having a wonderful evening, and I have you to thank for that," he said.

She smiled as she nestled her head against his chest and took in another whiff of his intoxicating aroma.

Time passed too quickly and before long, she found herself back in the limo on the way home. The evening had been magical, and when Larson walked her to the door, all she could do was wonder if he would kiss her goodnight. As he leaned in, to kiss her, his cell phone rang.

"Savannah, I'm so sorry, but I need to take this call it's the office."

Larson answered the phone to hear "Hello, Larson, this is your mother."

"What can I do for you, Mother?"

"Well, you can start by telling me what you're doing with that girl?"

"Are you following me, Mother?"

"Me, follow you? Sorry, son, I have people who do that."

"For the last time, what can I do for you, Mother?"

"You can stop wasting your time, and hers, we both know this will end in disaster."

"This conversation is over, Mother. Goodbye."

Larson hung up, but his heart continued to pound with anger.

"Are you all right, Larson?"

He clenched his fist. "I'm fine," he finally said. Standing there, he could only think about what his mother had said. As he walked back toward her to say goodnight, he fought down his hesitation and leaned in to kiss her. She held him close as he kissed her passionately.

"Goodnight," he said as he pulled away, breathless. "I had a wonderful time."

"So did I," Savannah said as she closed the door between them.

Three

Larson arrived at his office at eight o'clock the next morning.

"Good morning, Mr. Mansfield."

"Good morning, Elise. Are there any messages for me?"

"Yes, sir, and a heads up; your mother's in your office."

"Elise, would you send flowers and candy to this address please, and hold my calls?"

When Larson walked in his office, Caroline was sitting behind his desk.

"Hello, Mother, you're in early."

"And it seems you're late."

"What can I help you with Mother?"

"Did you sleep at home last night?"

"If this meeting doesn't involve work, Mother, I'm busy."

"I called a board meeting for this afternoon; you just make sure you're there, Larson."

"I'll be there, if there's nothing else, I have work to do."

Larson sat at his desk thinking about his evening with Savannah. He had never met anyone who made him feel the way she did, and he wanted her to know how remarkable their evening had been.

* * *

Savannah was still in her pajamas enjoying her morning coffee when the doorbell rang. There in the doorway stood a young man with the most beautiful bouquet of flowers and candy.

"*Bonjour*, Ms. Monreaux?"

"Yes."

"These are for you, *mademoiselle*."

"Thank you."

The flowers were stunning. As Savannah open the card, she read. *Savannah, thank you for a wonderful evening, I hope to see you again soon, L.* She was so excited she felt a warm flush in her cheeks knowing Larson wanted to see her again. I have to tell someone, so she picked up the phone and called her best friend Justine.

"Hi, Justine, it's Savannah."

"Hey, how are things going in Paris?"

"Things are great," she said full of excitement.

"It's so good to hear from you," said Justine.

Savannah began to tell her about her date with Larson.

They had so much fun she hadn't noticed they had been on the phone for almost an hour. "Well, Justine, we'd better say good night, or in your case good morning."

"Savannah, Larson sounds like a wonderful guy, but promise you won't get too close too fast."

"I won't."

But in her heart she knew she'd already fallen for him.

* * *

Savannah hung up the phone and headed to the bathroom to wash up. She had just drawn a bath when there was a knock at the door.

"Who is it?" Savannah asked.

"Caroline Mansfield."

Savannah's heart sank.

What could she possibly want? And how did she know where to find me? Savannah opened the door slowly.

"Hello, Mrs. Mansfield. What are you doing here?"

"May I come in?" said Caroline.

Savannah stepped aside allowing Caroline to enter.

"Savannah, without wasting too much of our time, I'm going to come right out with it; I'm here about my son."

"Your son, I'm afraid I don't understand."

"Listen, I understand things move a little slower where you're from so let me spell it out for you; you're, not the right woman for my son."

Savannah stood speechless for a moment. "Mrs. Mansfield, whatever it is you think is going on with your son I can assure you, we are just getting to know one another."

Caroline, noticing the flowers and candy asked, "Are these from my son?"

Reluctant to answer Savannah said, "Yes," as she began to smile.

"Don't flatter yourself," said Caroline, "he would do that for any woman after a night out."

"I don't think I like what you're implying," said Savannah. "I'm sorry, but I'm going to have to ask you to leave."

"I'm only trying to spare you the heartache that will surely come to you later," said Caroline.

"Goodbye, Mrs. Mansfield," Savannah said as she closed the door behind her. She could feel her face getting warm. She'd never been so angry, and without notice, the tears began to pour. Upset and shaking she wondered what had just happened. This morning she was so happy about her date last night. Justine had just warned her not to fall to fast, maybe she was right.

The sound of the phone ringing startled her. What

if it were Larson? She couldn't bear to hear his voice right now. The phone rang, once, twice, three times, and then stopped. She took a deep breath saw the flowers and started sobbing again. The phone rang most of the day, but Savannah never answered; instead she stayed in bed with the curtains drawn.

* * *

Back at the office, Larson began closing out his work day. He'd been calling Savannah all afternoon and couldn't get her on the phone. Upon leaving the office, he decided to try Savannah once more, but again there was no answer. He began to worry, he'd been calling all day, and it was late.

As a last resort, he requested his chauffeur drive him to Savannah's chateau. As the limousine pulled up, Larson wondered if she hadn't had a good time last night and didn't have the heart to tell him. He approached the door and knocked. There was no answer, so he knocked a second and third time. Just as, he began to walk away, he heard Savannah's voice.

"Who is it?"

"It's me, Larson, may I come in? I've been calling all day I'm worried about you."

She cracked the door a bit.

"Hi, Larson, I'm sorry I'm not feeling well, can I call you tomorrow."

Larson could tell something was not right in her voice.

"Savannah, please forgive me if I did something wrong last night."

Unable to hold back the tears, she opened the door and began to cry.

"Savannah, what's wrong? Please talk to me."

As she looked into his beautiful green eyes, all she could think of was Caroline's visit. How could she tell him what happen with his mom, what if he wouldn't believe her? What if it turned him away? She took in a deep breath, "Larson, please, we need to talk." With a look of concern on his face, he sat down.

"I got a visit from your mother today."

"What?" he asked, standing up again, "My mother what? How did she even know where to find you?"

"I'm not sure, but she made it very clear, I am not the right woman for her son."

"What?" By now he'd begun shouting. Savannah had seen that particular shade of red before on Larson's face; the same day he'd gotten the upsetting phone call.

"Savannah, I'm so sorry; my mother has a way of getting under my skin. I promise you, those are her feelings, not mine, and I *will* deal with her later. Savannah, I care for you and last night was one of the best nights I've had in many years."

He raised his hand and gently wiped the tears from her cheek.

"Have you had anything to eat, Savannah?"

"I really haven't had much of an appetite today,

Larson."

"What if, I call out for some dinner and a bottle of wine, so we can talk?"

Larson continued to apologize for his mother's earlier visit. He and Savannah laughed and ate as Larson tried to make everything all right.

"Savannah, I know I've been saying this all night, but I truly am sorry."

"'It's, okay, Larson. I understand."

"No, Savannah, I'm afraid you don't, I really have never met anyone like you."

"Is that a good thing?" she asked.

"Yes, you're different, but in a good way."

"What way is that? Ordinary?" Savannah sighed.

"We both know there's nothing ordinary about you."

He leaned in and before she knew it his soft warm lips touched hers. She didn't resist. She liked the way he held her in his arms. When he pulled away, her eyes stayed closed, and her head spun, but not from the consumption of the wine they'd both had. Larson made her feel things. Things she couldn't control. Things she'd never felt before. She knew she'd be leaving soon, and it would break her heart to say goodbye. She didn't want her memories of France to be of a broken heart.

She gently pulled away, saying, "Larson, I have to leave soon, I don't want to become just another memory." Gazing into his eyes, she could feel her heart pounding. She had feelings for him, more than she'd ever had for any man.

"Savannah, I care a great deal for you, and I don't want to confuse you in any way."

She gently stroked his cheek with the back of her hand as she reached over and kissed him, softly at first, then with intense passion. He cradled her against his body as he whispered. "Are you sure?"

She didn't resist, kissing him again. He lifted her and carried her into the bedroom, then laid her gently on the bed. As she looked up at him, all she could think about was how much she desired him, and how handsome he was. He lay next to her brushing the hair from her face.

He asked again. "Are you sure?"

"Yes," she said as he began to kiss her neck while his large fingers unbuttoned her blouse.

* * *

The next morning, Savannah woke to an empty bed. Larson had gone, but in his place left a note, and a red rose.

It read:

Savannah,

The more time we spend together, the more I learn about myself. Thank you for a beautiful night. I will pick you up tonight at 7:00 p.m. for dinner. I have a surprise for you.

Larson.

She smiled. The smell of his cologne lingered on the bedding. She breathed in deeply and wrapped the sheets around her. He'd been her first. She'd had male friends before, but it had never gone this far. She'd wanted her first time to be special, and Larson had made that happen. He'd been gentle, loving, and made her feel as though this was his first time, even though she knew it wasn't.

Her time in France would end soon, and she'd allowed herself to fall in love. In love, she thought, is that what I am? It had to be, she wouldn't have given herself to anyone else.

* * *

Caroline sat in the kitchen waiting for Larson.

"You've been out all night, care to tell me who with?"

"That's none of your concern, Mother, and after the way you treated Savannah, I'm surprised, she let me in."

"So you slept with her?"

"This conversation is over, Mother."

"This is far from over, son," she mumbled.

As Larson left the room, Caroline called for Charles, telling him to bring the limo around; she had an errand to run.

"Where would you like to go, Mrs. Mansfield?" asked Charles.

49

"There's a problem I need to take care of."

* * *

Larson headed to the study calling out for Caroline.

"Mother, I said I need to speak with you," but all he could hear was the remnant of his own voice. Deciding to go home, he planned an evening out for Savannah and him. He would pour out his heart to her and tell her how he truly felt. Tell her exactly what she means to him. He made reservations at his favorite restaurant as he jumped into the shower for their special evening.

* * *

Savannah was still glowing from her night with Larson. She'd met the most wonderful man, and dreaded how soon she had to return home.

Savannah watched the huge car pull up. She still jumped at the sound of the knock on the door.

"Mrs. Mansfield, I'm surprised to see you." In truth, Savannah's heart seemed to pound in her throat. Caroline had come to her room yesterday, and the unpleasantness of her visit still struck fear in Savannah. Once she caught her breath, she asked?

"What are you doing here? What can I do for you?"

"What can you do for me?" Caroline sneered at Savannah. "Why, nothing of course. But I'm going to do you a favor. I'm going to give you one more chance to stay away from my son."

"And why should I do that? Are those Larson's wishes?" Savannah asked.

"No, they are not," said Caroline, laughing as she said it. "You think because he spent the night you're special? Before you board the plane back to that one horse town you came from, you will be nothing more than a memory." Caroline turned, and as she walked out the door said, "Don't make trouble for yourself, Savannah; I'm not always this pleasant."

Savannah stood in the doorway, furious. She replayed Caroline's words in her mind. Did she just threaten me? She stood for a moment, unable to move. Why is this happening? Why does she hate me?

Savannah called home. She needed to hear her mother's voice. Talking to her mother, she filled her in on what had happened with Caroline.

"Savannah, why is she treating you this way? What happened?"

"Nothing, I swear, nothing at all."

Savannah started to cry, and was sobbing so hard, she could hardly breathe.

"Savannah, there are only a few days left to your trip, why don't you come home. I hate hearing you upset."

She thought about how hard it would be to say goodbye to Larson. Maybe this would be for the best; she'd fallen for him, and it would break her heart to say goodbye; but her recent visit from Caroline had left a bitter taste in her mouth. Realizing Caroline would never accept her with Larson, she hung up with her mother, and began to pack. She called the airline, changed her ticket, and before she knew it was in a cab on her way to the airport.

* * *

Larson waited in the foyer of his mother's house. He wanted to surprise Savannah. "Charles I need transportation to Ms. Monreaux's, please."

"Sure thing, Mr. Mansfield this will be my second time to Ms. Savannah's today."

"What do you mean the second-time today?"

"I took your mother there earlier today, sir."

Panic overtook Larson with such intensity he could barely breathe.

"Get me to Ms. Monreaux's, Charles. Now!"

Four

Larson shoved open the car door before the limo came to a full stop. He rushed out of the car and to the door. He knocked on the door hoping Savannah would answer, but no one came.

"Maybe she's out? I should have called first," he mumbled. He hurried to the lobby to inquire about Savannah.

"Hello, my name is Larson Mansfield, I'm here to see Ms. Monreaux in room 6B."

"I'm sorry, sir," said the attendant, "but Ms. Monreaux checked out several hours ago."

"Checked out? Did she say where she was going?"

"The airport I believe, back home to the states, sir."

Larson suddenly felt sick to his stomach. She'd gone, and all he could think about was getting her back. He remembered in their conversations she'd spoken of her hometown in the U.S. some place called Louisiana where she lived in a small town called Carencro.

What had his mother said to her to make her leave so suddenly? Larson called the airport checking every recent flight out to the states. All flights were on time, and gone.

* * *

Savannah trudged through the airport toward her plane. She swiped at her eyes, burning and swollen from all the crying she'd done. Once on the plane, she took her seat, closed her eyes, and immediately saw Larson's face. She would miss him and knew her heart would ache for him, but her leaving was for the best.

"Please put your trays in an upright position."

Before she could second-guess her decision, the plane leveled off among the clouds.

* * *

Caroline sat in the study gloating over her recent visit with Savannah. "Not my son," she said aloud grinning. "No, *poubelle sud* will ever have the last name Mansfield, not while I'm alive."

"She is *not* southern trash, Mother!"

Caroline startled at the angry tone of her son's voice.

"What is it, Larson?" asked Caroline, "You don't have to shout."

"Mother, what did you do? What did you say to

Savannah?"

Refusing to cower before her son, Caroline stood. "I told her the truth, something you should have told her yourself if you weren't so weak."

"I won't ask again, what did you say to her?"

"I told her she would never be a member of this family, she would not be a Mansfield."

She flinched when Larson threw the glass he'd been drinking from. The glass shattered showering shards and liquid everywhere.

"You do *not* speak for me, Mother. You have no right."

"Calm down, Larson. I did you a favor. What did you imagine would happen, the two of you would get married have a house with a white picket fence and little *poubelle sud* babies running around? This is not her world, and it is better you see that now before it's too late."

"You speak of her, as though she's unintelligent and uneducated. Well, she's neither."

"You're thinking with your male trophy again, Larson, and we both know that won't last."

Larson turned, storming out of the house.

"Where are you going?" asked Caroline.

"Anywhere but here," he said slamming the door behind him.

* * *

Savannah's plane had been in the air for eight

hours now, and she was anxious to get home. She wondered if Larson had tried to call, she should have told him about her leaving. She felt miserable, maybe she should have explained why, but that would have only prolonged things. The more she thought about it, the more she realized it was better this way. After several plane changes, and a murderous fifteen and a half hours Savannah's plane finally landed in New Orleans. Her mother and father stood waiting for her at baggage.

"Savannah, it's so good to see you," said Adele. What have you done to your hair?"

"Do you like it, Mom?" asked Savannah.

"Like it. I love it. You look amazing."

"Hi, Dad."

"Oh boy, my baby girl has grown into a beautiful woman it seems, overnight."

Her father kissed her on the cheek grabbed her bags, and they headed toward the car. Savannah stayed quiet on the ride home, though her mother tried to make conversation she knew that her daughter was hurting, and didn't want to push her. Exhausted from her flight, Savannah had fallen asleep. She woke to the soft touch of her mother's hand on her arm.

"Are you sure you want to stay alone at your apartment tonight?"

"Yes."

"You know, we have your old room fixed with

fresh linens. You could stay the night with us."

"Thanks, Mom, what I really want is to go home and get settled in."

"Savannah if you need us we are only a few minutes away," said Adele.

He father put the bags inside as Savannah, and her mother said goodnight. Savannah went inside, closed the door, and retreated to her bedroom, falling onto the bed exhausted.

* * *

Larson sat at home starting his second drink hoping the more he drank, the more he could forget. However, just the opposite had happened, and he could not erase the image of Savannah's face. Several drinks later, his head grew so heavy he couldn't hold it up any longer. He settled back and passed out.

He awoke the next morning to the ringing of the phone and an ache in his head almost as bad as the one in his heart.

He looked at the caller ID and decided not to answer. He had no intention of speaking with his mother. The answering machine picked up. *Sorry I'm unavailable, Please leave a message and I will get back with you.*

"Larson, this is your mother, pick up the phone I know you're home."

He didn't answer. She waited, and then hung up. His head felt as though it had been rolled over by a steam truck. He went to the cabinet and got something for the pain. However, before the pills were down his throat, he was thinking of Savannah again. He wouldn't be going into work today or maybe even the rest of the week. He needed time off, time to get his thoughts right. His mother be damned.

* * *

Savannah started another day with a headache and swollen eyes. She'd cried herself to sleep again last night, and promised herself it would not happen again. She would be returning to work on Monday, and all she needed to do was relax.

Over the next few days, Savannah took her time to unpack it seemed everything reminded her of France. She put away the souvenirs she'd bought for everyone, they only reminded her of her visit. She slept most of the weekend, and before she knew it Monday crept up.

Oh how I hate Mondays. She'd worked for Eduard, Clement, & Frederic LLP, an accounting firm for almost ten years. Her bosses were hard, but fair, and happy with her work. She got a pay raise every year, as did any who proved themselves, along with bonuses when the company excelled.

She sat at her desk, ready to work, but an image of Larson came to mind. *We've settled this it's over, so get out of my head.*

The rest of the day went well, with the occasional fire that needed putting out. She and Justine were so busy they hardly had a chance to talk.

"Justine, I have so much to tell you about my trip, but we'll have to catch up later."

"No problem. I'm swamped with work as well; we'll talk later."

Five o'clock came; Savannah shut down her computer locked her office and left for home.

* * *

Larson sat in his living room nursing his hangover. He'd ignored his mother's phone calls the last few days. Finally needing to eat, he called out for something, and poured himself something to drink.

"I think I'll stick with tea, and water the rest of the night," he said.

He decided to get on the computer and try and get some work done, even though he wasn't going into the office. While, on the computer, he did a search to look up information about the town where Savannah said she lived. What did she say that name was? Carencro, that's it, Carencro, Louisiana. He put in the name and pressed search. Information about the town's history and culture came up, along with population and other statistics. Larson read through the material, becoming so fascinated by what he read he, lost track of time. Carencro was a town with working-class people of multi-cultural ethnicity; which is one of the things he loved about Savannah. He did a search of the phone listing for Savannah Monreaux; to his surprise, he found a few. There were middle initials and middle names, but he suddenly realized he had never asked her middle name. He printed out the list, and laid it aside. "I'll check on it later."

* * *

Caroline paced her study. She still hadn't heard from Larson, all of her phone calls went unanswered.

"Charles, please bring the car around; I'm going to find Larson."

Some time later, Caroline pounded her fist against her son's door. "Who is it?"

Caroline didn't answer for fear he wouldn't open the door.

"Who is it?" Larson said again, frustration clear in his tone.

"It's your mother, open the door."

"Not today, Mother, I don't have the patience, or the time."

"Look, I'm worried about you; I just need to know you're all right."

"I'm fine, Mother now go home."

"At least let me apologize for my behavior, then I promise I'll leave."

Larson opened the door, against his better judgment.

"Hello, Mother. What do you have to say?"

"I'm sorry about my behavior. I was simply trying to do what I thought best. I just didn't want her to be

60

hurt or embarrassed; your lives are very different. I'm only trying to help; I never meant to hurt her." She looked at Larson with tears in her eyes and said, "Can you ever forgive me?"

He looked back at his mother saying, "On one condition, Mother, we need to set some boundaries."

"As you wish."

"I need you to stay out of my private life. If you can't do that, we are wasting our time here."

Caroline agreed and kissed her son on the cheek.

"So when will you be coming back to work?"

"I'm not sure," he said, "but it won't be tomorrow."

"Maybe you should consider coming back soon, it will keep your mind off things," pushed Caroline.

He knew she was right, all he had done at home was beat himself up about Savannah, and going to work would undoubtedly redirect all of that.

"I'll think about it," he said.

She said goodbye as she walked out the door.

In the hallway, she stopped for a moment. *That went well. I should get an Academy Award for the display of gibberish I just spewed.*

Five

Things settled back to normal for Savannah. She kept busy at work, which helped to distract her from her recent trip to France. The weeks went by more quickly, and she had started to put the past behind her. The weekend was on its way and Savannah and her mother had planned a day together. They would have a girl's night out, dinner and a movie. She loved spending time with her mother. They'd always been more like best friends than mother and daughter. They could talk about anything, but Savannah wasn't ready to talk about what happened in France between her and Larson, though she knew her mother would ask.

* * *

Larson was still trying to figure out the motives behind his mother's visit. He knew her well enough not to think she'd meant anything she'd said when she apologized. He looked at the list of phone numbers he'd found on the Internet. He missed Savannah, and wanted to hear her voice. He had no idea what he would say to her after what had transpired with his mother. He wanted to call, but what if she didn't want to speak to him. Picking up the phone, he dialed the first number. By the fourth number, he'd decided to give up. He moved to disconnect until someone answered.

"Hello," said a soft familiar voice.

Larson felt his throat starting to close on him.

"Hello," again said the voice on the other end of the line.

"Savannah," he said nervously.

After what seemed like an eternity she said, "Larson, is that you?"

"Yes, Savannah, it's me. I'm so sorry for calling. If you want me to hang up, I will, but I really wanted to talk to you."

"Larson, are you all right; what time is it there?"

"Its 3:00 a.m., I couldn't sleep. The truth is, Savannah, I haven't been myself since you left." He thought back to those many nights of hangovers. "Can we talk? Are you busy?"

"Sure," she said sounding excited.

Larson cleared his throat. "I'm not quite sure where to begin. I want you to know, I had no idea my mother had gone by the chateau to see you until she'd done it."

He told her about the plans he'd made for that evening, and how he'd wanted to surprise her. He paused for a moment and took a deep breath, releasing it heavily into the phone.

"Savannah, I went to the chateau because I needed to tell you something."

It suddenly got quite on the phone.

"What is it, Larson?" asked Savannah.

Larson tried to speak again, but the words didn't seem to come. Finally, he said, "You have somehow taken hold of my heart in a way I don't want to live without. I can't stop thinking about you, and can't bear the thought of never seeing or hearing from you again."

Savannah didn't say anything and Larson hoped with all his heart that she felt the same way.

"What will you do about your mother?" she asked.

He didn't want to tell her about his conversation with Caroline. He knew her apology meant nothing, and she wouldn't be happy if she knew he'd called.

"Look, Savannah, I know my mother, and she won't be happy about this, but I am determined to make this work."

Larson noticed the time, but didn't care.

"Larson, you have to be at work in a few hours and I have to get some sleep, can we talk later?"

"Sure, I'm sorry for keeping you up."

"Don't worry about me," she said "I don't have to

be at work for a while."

Larson laughed.

"What's so funny?" she asked.

"I forgot to tell you, I took some days off work; I needed to clear my head."

Savannah laughed as well. "Well I'd better get to bed then."

Larson hung up the phone feeling relieved, Savannah had allowed him to speak, and showed no signs of regret. She didn't seem too upset by her visits from Caroline. Of course, she'd been upset enough to leave without a word, but he understood.

* * *

Caroline arrived home feeling triumphant. Larson had obviously accepted her apology as sincere and everything in the Mansfield household would be fine.

* * *

A month passed with Larson and Savannah speaking almost every night. Things seemed to be going great between them; they emailed each other as often as they spoke. Savannah found herself falling in love all over again, but Caroline hovered in the back of her mind. They'd decided to keep their conversations and relationship to themselves. She hadn't even told her mother, which had started to cause her pain. She had never kept anything from her mom and hated she hadn't opened up to her. Savannah decided if things continued to move in a positive direction, only then would she tell her mother.

Wednesday morning Savannah woke up tired. For some reason, she hadn't been feeling well. A nasty bug had made its way around the office, and she'd finally come down with it. She dragged herself out of bed and got into the shower. With no appetite, she skipped breakfast. She threw on her jacket and headed out the door for work. When she got to work, she wasn't feeling any better.

"Good morning, Justine."

"Savannah, you don't look well. Are you all right?"

"I think I've got that bug everyone's been passing around."

"Girl, please don't get too close to me, I can't afford to get sick. Why didn't you stay home today, Savannah? You know you have the time, you never take off work." Justine looked sympathetic, but kept her distance.

"With me just getting back in the groove of things after vacation, I didn't want my work to start piling up again."

"Well, if you need anything just let me know."

"Thanks, Justine. Don't pretend you don't hear me calling you if I do."

They both laughed as Savannah went to her office to get on with her day. She suffered through the rest of morning. She didn't feel any better, but by the afternoon she could finally get some soup down. There were two emails from Larson waiting for her, but she'd been too busy most of the morning to check them until now.

Just thinking of you, hope you have a terrific day.

The brief note made her smile. She read the second note.

Working very late tonight, then a board meeting. I won't be in early; do you want to talk later?

She still wasn't feeling great, but didn't want to miss hearing his voice, so she sent an email back.

Good day, I hope yours is too, looking forward to our conversation, call whenever you get in.

Five o'clock finally arrived and Savannah headed out of the office.

"Goodbye, Savannah, if you're looking and feeling the way you did this morning, please don't come in tomorrow."

"I really just don't want to call in sick, Justine, you know I don't like missing work."

"I know, but even Mr. Frederic said you shouldn't have come into work today."

"Okay fine, if I feel this bad tomorrow I'll stay home."

"Good," said Justine, "we have enough people walking around here sick."

When Savannah got home, she called her mom to tell her she was ill and may not go into work tomorrow.

"Savannah, I'm coming over, I'll bring some fluids, and soup."

"Mom, I'm not really that hungry."

"Nonsense, Savannah, I'll go by the store, and pick up a few things, and then I'll be right over."

"Thanks, Mom." After hanging up the phone, she peeled off her clothes and went straight to bed. She didn't have the strength to shower; she would take one in the morning.

When her mom knocked on the door, it felt as though she'd just laid her head down for a nap. She got up opening the door for her mom.

"Mom, where's your key?"

"I have it, honey, but my hands are full."

She looked as though she'd picked up enough groceries for the month.

"Mom, what's all this? I'm not hungry."

"I figured you hadn't gone shopping since you returned from France."

She put the bag down and looked at Savannah.

"You look terrible. Are you running a fever?"

"No, Mom, I'm not running a fever, but everyone at work has been getting some kind of bug."

"Maybe you should go to the doctor, Savannah."

Not wanting to argue, Savannah tried to soothe her mother's concerns.

"I promise if I'm not better in a few days I'll go,

but all I want to do right now is get some rest."

"Well, you call me if you need me; I'm only a few minutes away."

"I will, Mom. Thank you so much for everything. I love you."

"I love you too, Savannah." With a pat on the arm, her mother left, closing the door behind her.

Later in the evening, Savannah had finally felt like eating and was thankful her mother had gone shopping. After dinner, she began to feel better, and decided to watch some television while she waited for Larson to call. She dozed off on the couch, and just as she began to dream, the phone rang. She snatched it up.

"Savannah, hi; did I wake you? You sound startled."

"Wow, no, I guess I fell asleep."

"Are you okay? You don't sound like yourself." Larson sounded worried.

"I've been feeling ill since yesterday," she said.

"I'm so sorry, is there anything I can do to help?"

"I'm sure there is, but not while you're in France." She laughed.

"Well, at least you still have your sense of humor."

"That's me, a funny girl. I know you're worried, but I'll be fine."

"I'll call to check on you tomorrow. Savannah, please don't try to go into work."

"I promise, if I feel this way tomorrow, I'll stay

home."

Larson paused before saying, "I miss you, and the more we talk, the harder it gets."

"I understand, I feel the same way, we'll talk tomorrow. Good night, Larson."

"Good night, Savannah."

* * *

The next day, Savannah stayed home and tried to nurse herself back to health. Her mom showed up and set to work trying to tidy up around the apartment. Her dad had also come by and fixed them both breakfasts. Savannah managed to keep it down, finally getting off the soup. She and her mom spent most of the morning talking. She'd finally felt comfortable enough to talk about her recent trip when the doorbell rang. Adele got up, answering the door.

"Is this Savannah Monreaux's residence?"

"Yes, it is," said Adele.

"These are for you," he said and walked away.

"Savannah, these must be for you, they're gorgeous. Quick, let's see who they're from."

Savannah already knew and wasn't ready to tell her mom that she and Larson had started talking again. She picked the card from the flowers, slowly opened it up, and said, "Oh, it's from work."

"Well, what does it say," asked Adele.

"It says hoping you are better soon."

"It was so nice of them to send you such beautiful

flowers."

Savannah tucked the card into her pocket and told her mom she would save it in her memory book. This way she wouldn't have to explain Larson's name on the card.

She hated lying to her mom. This was so unlike her, but what could she do.

Six

Larson sat in the parlor of his mother's house, his legs crossed. Caroline returned to her usual self, barking out orders to everyone while making them feel small and incompetent. Larson had arrived for dinner, trying to pretend everything was all right. He would not be dropping his guard with his mother, especially knowing her as he did. Dinner consisted of Caroline talking and Larson pretending to listen. His mind frequently drifted to Savannah. He wondered if she were feeling any better.

"Larson, are you listening to me?"

"What? Yes, I'm listening to you, Mother."

"Well pay attention, I ran into Lisette yesterday. She inquired about you."

"I'm not interested in seeing Lisette."

"Well, that poses a problem. I've invited her over for dinner tomorrow night."

"Call and tell her I'm not available."

"I will do no such thing. Besides, I have no way of getting in touch with her. She'll be here around 7:00. Please try to be on time, we're having lobster."

Larson excused himself from the table saying he needed to get home. He truly just missed Savannah and wanted to check in on her. As he began to walk out the door, Caroline yelled out, "Don't forget to be here before 7:00 tomorrow."

Larson was already regretting dinner. Caroline adored Lisette, one of his former girlfriends, mainly because they were just alike. He and Lisette had dated for three years. His mother pushed for a wedding, but he'd come to realize he and Lisette would never make each other happy.

Once home, he shed his clothes and jumped into the shower. As he settled onto the bed to call Savannah, he realized he was more tired than he'd thought. On the third ring he heard, "Hello, Larson, how are you?"

"I should be asking you that question. How are you feeling?"

"I finally kept something down today, but I'm still not feeling any better."

"Savannah, remember you promised if you weren't feeling better by tomorrow you'd go to the doctor."

"I promise. Now that we've cleared that up, I want to thank you for the flowers. They're breathtaking."

"I just wanted to make your day a little brighter, since you weren't feeling well."

"Well it worked. So tell me, how was your day?"

"Busy," he answered. He wasn't sure he should tell her about Lisette, especially since there was little to tell.

"Just out of curiosity, Larson, how is your mother now that I'm gone?"

"The same, as meddlesome as ever, but there's something I want to tell you."

"What is it, Larson?"

He told her about his mother inviting Lisette to dinner tomorrow night. He explained to her about their relationship long ago.

"I'm really sorry, but I can assure you, Savannah, any feelings that were there, are long gone."

He endured the silence on the phone for a moment until Savannah finally said, "Larson, I trust you. It's your mother's motives that bother me. Let's face it; she'll do anything to make sure I'm not in the picture."

"Which is exactly why she mustn't know anything," he said.

"I don't like the idea of lying, Larson, but I trust you to do what's best."

"Thank you, Savannah. That means a lot."

"Larson, I would love to talk more, but I'm really tired. I think it's time for a nap."

Concerned that she might be trying to get rid of

him, he tried to encourage her. "Savannah, please don't worry. I assure you my heart is truly where it wants to be."

"I believe you. We'll talk again soon."

Larson disconnected the call, but was too wound up to fall asleep. He laid there trying to decide what to do next.

* * *

Savannah slept through the rest of that afternoon straight through to morning. She woke up feeling sick again.

"Darn, I thought I was getting better, but this just won't quit."

Everyone at work had gotten over the illness in two to three days. She'd now been sick for four. "Okay, a promise is a promise." She got her doctor's number and called.

"Dr. Broussard's office may I help you."

"This is Savannah Monreaux; I was hoping Dr. Broussard had an opening for today." She explained how sick she'd been, and that she really needed to see the doctor.

"Ms. Monreaux, we'll work you in, just come to the office."

"Thank you so much. I'll be there in fifteen minutes." She called to let her mom know she would be going to the doctor's office. Adele wanted to go with her, but Savannah explained she was fine and would call when she got home saying it had to be the bug from work. She hung up the phone then headed out the door. Arriving at the office, Savannah found herself in good spirits. She would get something for this bug, and be back to work in no time. Savannah sat in the waiting room until the nurse called her name.

"Good morning, Ms. Monreaux, what seems to be the problem?"

Savannah explained her symptoms to the nurse and that she'd started feeling crummy after returning to work from her trip to France.

"I think I've caught what everyone else has been passing around the office."

"Please have a seat, Ms. Monreaux; Dr. Broussard will be with you shortly. For now, I need you to put on this robe."

"Thank you." Savannah struggled into the gown which seemed at least two sizes too small.

"Why can't they make these things, so they fit?" she mumbled.

She pulled it shut as much as possible while waiting for the doctor. A tap on the door startled her.

"Hello, Ms. Monreaux. I've looked over your chart. Let's see if we can find out what's going on."

He began the examination pressing and poking, asking if she hurt anywhere. Savannah explained her biggest problem was keeping food in her stomach and being extra tired.

"Well, Ms. Monreaux, you're not running a temperature and you're not having the same symptoms as the other patients I've seen with the virus that's been going around. We'll take some blood work, and see what's going on. I should have the results for you tomorrow. For now I want you to take this, it will settle your stomach and help with the nausea. I want you to stay hydrated as well," he said as he walked out the door.

"Savannah," said the nurse, "I'll be right back to get your blood work. You can go ahead and get dressed now."

The nurse prepped her arm for the blood draw. Once she inserted the needle, she waited while several vials filled. "Wow, how much blood are you taking?"

The nurse laughed, saying, "I promise we won't take it all."

When the nurse finished, she told Savannah she was free to go, and they would call her tomorrow with the results.

Savannah left the office, but it was going to be a long night. She hated waiting for test results, even though she knew she had nothing to worry about. She called her mom on the way home, filling her in on her conversation with the doctor and letting her know she'd have the results tomorrow.

* * *

Later that night, Larson called, checking to see if

77

she felt any better.

"So what did the doctor say, Savannah? Is it that bug, from work?"

"He didn't think so; he said the symptoms weren't the same as the other patients, so he's running some blood work."

Larson tried to comfort her, saying it would be fine and she shouldn't worry. She agreed as they said an early goodnight.

The next morning Savannah woke early so she could call into work. It was a few minutes before 8:00 she dialed the phone.

"Eduard, Clement, and Frederic how may I help you?"

"Justine, its Savannah."

"Hey, girl, how are you doing? Are you still feeling bad?"

"It comes and goes, it seems just when I'm feeling better this thing starts up again. I'm waiting to hear from the doctor's office today about the blood work, so hopefully I'll be in soon."

Justine told her to hurry back everyone missed her at the office. Savannah paced around the house most of the day, worrying, until finally the phone rang.

"Hello, Ms. Monreaux, this is Dr. Broussard's secretary, he would like you to come into the office today."

"Come in? Is there something wrong? Don't you

normally just give these types of results over the phone?"

"I'm sorry, Ms. Monreaux, but that's as much as I can tell you. Are you available to come into the office?"

"Yes," she said with a worrisome sigh, "I'll be right in."

"Thank you, just check in at the desk when you get here."

Why do I have to go in? What did they see in those blood tests? She worried all the way to the office. Pulling up to the office she remembered she hadn't called her mom to tell her she'd be at the doctor's office. She decided it would be best to wait. Besides, she actually had no idea if anything were wrong.

"Hi, Savannah Monreaux, here to see doctor Broussard," she said as she checked in at the front desk.

"Yes, Ms. Monreaux, we've been waiting for you. Please have a seat, it should only be a minute."

The secretary was right, it had only been a few minutes when doctor Broussard called her in. Savannah was so scared she'd begun to shake and to make matters worse she'd become nauseated again. As Dr. Broussard looked at her file, she couldn't keep it in any longer.

Savannah dropped down into a chair. "Dr. Broussard, is there something wrong with me?" Am I

79

going to die? Is it bad news?"

"Calm down, Savannah, you're not going to die, I can promise you, and it's not bad news."

"Why did I have to come in? What's wrong with me?"

"Ms. Monreaux, I'll be referring you to Dr. Martin who will be following your progress."

"Dr. Martin, what kind of doctor is he?"

"He, Ms. Monreaux, is a she, and a gynecologist. I'll be referring you to *her*. She'll be following your pregnancy."

"My what?" Savannah shot out of her chair. She stood waiting for the punch line.

"You're with child, Ms. Monreaux. This is wonderful news, smile."

She found little comfort in knowing that what she had wasn't going to kill her, but what was she going to do? What would her parents say? What about Larson and Caroline? All these things swam around in her head until she nearly fainted.

"Are you all right, Ms. Monreaux?" Dr. Broussard gestured toward a chair. "Sit here for a minute; we'll get you some water."

The doctor called the nurse in to check Savannah's blood pressure.

"*Hmm*, a little high. I'm afraid you'll have to stay until we can get your pressure down. Try and relax. We'll be in again in a few minutes."

All Savannah could think about was Larson.

The doctor returned to the room, checking her blood pressure again which had gone back to normal. Dr. Broussard told Savannah she could go, but not before he asked, "Ms. Monreaux, was this a planned pregnancy?"

Savannah shook her head.

"Most of my patients are ecstatic when I tell them they're pregnant. That doesn't seem to be the case in your situation. If you need help with options, Dr. Martin will have information available for you."

She got up slowly, said thank you, and walked out the door. When she got to her car, all she could do was cry. What was she going to do? She couldn't even contemplate the notion of doing anything to harm her child. She regained her composure and drove home.

Seven

Larson arrived at his mother's house at exactly 7:00 o'clock, none too happy about this dinner his mother had forced upon him. Besides, he was worried about Savannah; she'd been on his mind all day. There'd been no word yet on the doctor's appointment. He'd tried calling her but got no response. He entered the house as Charles took his coat.

"Your mother and Ms. Lisette are waiting in the sitting room." He leaned in. "They've finished a bottle of wine already."

Larson sighed. "Thank you, Charles."

"Dinner will be served momentarily, sir," said Charles.

As Larson walked into the dining area he heard his mother's voice.

"Larson, it's so nice of you to be on time."

"Hello, Mother, how are you?"

"I'm fine, dear. You remember Lisette, don't you?"

"Of course, he remembers me," said Lisette "we dated long enough. I just never could get him to commit."

"Hello, Lisette, you're looking well, how have you been feeling?"

"Lonely, but suddenly refreshed," she said with a smile. "So how has work been treating you?"

"Busy, Lisette, very busy."

"Don't sell yourself short son," said Caroline. "Larson is now CEO and has proven to be quite worthy of the title."

"Really, well it's not surprising you were always the most business savvy person I knew."

"Yes," said Caroline, "it's just a shame, him working so hard with no time for female companionship."

"Well now that just won't do." Lisette smiled again. "So am I to understand there is no one special in your life?"

Larson wanted so badly to shout that he'd found the most wonderful girl in the world, but just as, the words were about to slip from his tongue, he caught himself.

"Dinner is now served," interrupted Charles.

Dinner was spent with Lisette throwing herself at Larson, and Caroline trying to get them together.

"Larson, you're still as handsome as I remember,"

said Lisette.

Caroline excused herself from the table saying she'd be right back, but Larson recognized his mother's ploy to leave him and Lisette alone. Lisette moved closer to Larson's seat.

"You know, Larson; I never quite got over you, and still think of you often. Do you think maybe there's a chance we could try again?"

"Trying again is not on my list of things to do with you, Lisette," he said in an agitated tone.

"Why not? We're both adults in need of some intimate pleasure. When was the last time you felt the soft caress of a women's hand?"

Larson remembered that night with Savannah and smiled.

"What's this?" said Lisette. "You look as if there is someone?"

Larson remained silent, not wanting to raise any suspicion.

Finally, he said, "There's no one, Lisette. I'm fine on my own."

Lisette leaned in toward him saying, "We both know that's not true, or you wouldn't be so frustrated."

Caroline returned to the dining room saying, "I'm so sorry for my absence, it couldn't be helped. I hope you two have had some time to get reacquainted." Larson stood suddenly saying, "I'm terribly sorry, but I have some business to attend to."

"Business," said Caroline, "it can wait until tomorrow."

Larson kissed his mother on the cheek, and turned toward Lisette saying, "Lisette, always a pleasure, and I hope you enjoy your time here in France."

Caroline fumed as he left the room. He stopped out of sight and listened. "Give him time. He'll come around."

"I'm not so sure," said Lisette.

"What do you mean?"

"I fear another may have taken hold of his heart." Lisette sighed.

"What makes you say that?"

"I'm not sure, but he definitely seems preoccupied by something."

Larson knew his mother would be thinking of Savannah, but not in the same way he was. He would have to keep his guard up. His mother summoned Charles to bring them another bottle of wine and assured Lisette someone would drive her back to her hotel.

Not wanting to be noticed, Larson quietly left the house and headed home. He needed to hear her voice.

* * *

Savannah couldn't stop shaking. How could she be pregnant? Well, she knew how, but *how*. She stared at the card given to her by Dr. Broussard and remembered what he'd said. She had no intentions of doing anything to harm her child, but she knew she needed a doctor. She picked up the phone, dialed the number, and waited for an answer.

"Hello, Dr. Martin's office."

"Hello, this is Savannah Monreaux, and I've been given Dr. Martin's name as a contact for *OBGYN* care."

Savannah listened as the woman on the phone asked a series of questions. After several minutes, the receptionist said they would see her the next morning at ten o'clock. Savannah hung up the phone and noticed she had messages. The first was from her mom, she sat there not knowing what to do. She had to call her back, or she'd be worried, but what would she tell her? Savannah picked up the phone and dialed the number. At first she could barely feel her fingers, then her whole body went numb.

When she called her mom, she answered the phone abruptly. "Savannah, I'm so glad it's you, I've been worried, Are you all right? What did the doctor say?"

"Calm down, Mom, the doctor said I'll be fine. I've gotten the bug from work. I'll only be out of work for a few more days, that's all."

She hated not telling her mother the truth.

"I'm glad, Savannah, I was so worried."

"Well, stop worrying, I'm fine."

"You certainly sound better," said Adele, asking if she'd had anything to eat.

Savannah told her mom her appetite was getting better, but she'd better stay on soup a while longer. While talking on the phone with her mother, a call came in from Larson.

"I have to get this call, Mom. I'll talk with you later."

"Hello, Larson."

"Savannah," a familiar, sweet voice said, "did I catch you at a bad time?"

"No, not at all," she said, hoping he wouldn't remember her recent appointment to the doctor's office.

"So what did the doctor say? I've been worried all afternoon."

She didn't want to lie to him. Her heart ached for not knowing what to do, and before she even realized it said, "Oh, it's nothing just that bug from work." She hung her head, ashamed for what she'd done to the man who had stolen her heart.

"That's great, Savannah, you'll be yourself again in no time."

Savannah agreed, and quickly changed the subject.

"So how was dinner at your mother's house?" she asked Larson, hoping he'd say what she wanted to hear.

"Dreadful, and to top it off, mother played matchmaker the whole time, leaving me alone with Lisette."

"Really, I'm sure it wasn't that bad. So what's she like? What did you guy's talk about?"

Larson laughed, saying, "Do I detect a bit of jealousy?"

"Of course not," she said smiling, "so what was she like?"

"The same as when we dated, self-centered and vain."

"Well is she still beautiful? And be honest."

"Well, if I have to be honest, yes she is."

Savannah got extremely quiet, she thought about the baby.

"Savannah," said Larson, "I miss you in a way I can't explain. It's as though I'm on this road at an intersection, and I'm trying to decide which way to go, but no matter what path I take it always leads to you."

Tears welled up in her eyes. She wanted to tell him the truth, but what if he wasn't ready for a child. Of course, there's also Caroline to worry about.

"Savannah, did you hear what I said?"

"I'm sorry; I guess I'm still not feeling well."

"Savannah, I miss you." He sounded sad. "Get some rest and we'll talk later."

Eight

Larson went to work early the next morning. He'd given up on getting any sleep. There was lots of work to do at the office, and he would be leaving soon for a one-month stay in England. Mansfield Enterprises were taking over a company there that had fallen short of profits for the last four years, and was sinking. Larson would be taking over for a month. He would re-staff, re-group, and turn it around for a profit. That's the way it worked, he had a knack for making businesses work. He'd be leaving in a few short days and had a lot to do before then.

"Mr. Mansfield," said Elise.

"Your mother would like to see you in her office."

"Tell her I'll be right there." He headed in that direction.

"You wanted to see me, Mother?"

"Yes, Larson, I wanted to know if you had a good

time at dinner last night."

"Mother, I'm really busy. I don't have time for this."

Larson had been through this the last time Caroline tried to get him and Lisette together. She was relentless, bringing Lisette over for dinner every chance she could.

"Larson, I'm only asking if you had a good time. What's wrong with that?"

"Nothing; I'm sorry, I'm just buried with work, I apologize, Mother."

"No need to apologize, son, I think this time away will be good for you. I know how you like rebuilding companies."

Larson nodded.

"So, when are you leaving? Do you need any help?" asked Caroline.

Larson would be leaving over the weekend; he was ready to get away from Caroline and Lisette. When he told his mother he was already packed and ready to go Caroline shouted, "Great, then you'll have time for dinner at our favorite restaurant tonight. How about I call Lisette to join us?"

Larson looked at his mother, he knew if he said no it would raise suspicion. "I was hoping to spend some quality time with my mother alone before leaving," he said.

"There's plenty of time for that," said Caroline,

"but how often do we get to see Lisette?"

Larson clenched his teeth as he agreed.

"So I'll set everything up for Friday night at eight. Lisette and I will meet you at seven with the limousine."

Larson walked out of his mother's office without saying anything else.

The phone rang once; then again until finally; he heard, "Hello."

"Savannah, are you busy?"

"Never too busy for you," she said.

"So how was your day?"

"So much better than yesterday," said Savannah.

"And the stomach bug, is it better?"

"Yes," she said.

"That's great; you'll be back at work in no time."

"Savannah I've really missed you."

"I've missed you, too, Larson."

They continued talking and laughing. Just as they were about to hang up, Caroline passed by the office.

"Larson, it's time to go you've done enough work today."

Larson pretended he was on the phone with business saying, "Thank you, sir, for your time, and I will get back to you soon."

Larson asked, "Mother, are you feeling all right? Your face is quite flushed."

"I'm fine," she said, but Larson could tell

something was wrong.

"Lisette and I will pick you up in the limousine for dinner." Larson sighed.

"Is that a problem?"

"No. No problem," he said quickly.

"Good, we will see you tonight for dinner."

* * *

Savannah had gone back to work, and for the most part she was back to normal except for the occasional queasiness. She and Dr. Martin had met and gone over all her options. She'd made her peace with knowing she might be raising her baby on her own.

Justine came to the office to check on Savannah and see if she needed anything.

"Savannah, are you okay?"

"Why do you ask? Don't I look okay?"

"Yes, you do, but you also look a bit preoccupied."

Savannah and Justine had been friends for a long time, and she hated not telling her what was going on. Besides, she truly needed someone she could talk to and trust.

"Justine, would you have dinner with me today? I really could use a friend."

"Of course, Savannah. I'll meet you here at twelve o'clock."

Savannah suddenly remembered the mix up between her and Larson about the difference between dinner and supper. She began to smile, putting her hand on her stomach while thinking of the love that had brought this marvelous creation to life.

Busy at work, Savannah spent most of the day playing catch up. Before she knew it, Justine was knocking on the door saying it was time to eat. At dinner, Savannah could barely eat, but thankfully Justine didn't push. They made small talk for a while.

Finally, Justine said, "Savannah, what did you want to talk about?" Savannah hung her head, taking in a deep breath.

"Do you remember how sick I was when I got back from France?"

Justine looked puzzled. "Of course I remember."

"I haven't been completely honest with you," said Savannah. "I'm really sorry; I didn't know what to do."

Justine looked at her, trying to figure out what might be wrong.

"I didn't have the bug from the office like everyone else."

"You didn't? So what did you have?"

Savannah looked up with tears in her eyes.

"What's wrong, Savannah? You know you can tell me anything."

"Justine, you have to promise you won't speak of this to anyone."

"Savannah, you're scaring me. What is it?"

She put her hands to her mouth and in a frail voice

said, "I'm pregnant."

Justine's eyes grew to the size of quarters. "You're what?" she asked, still processing the information.

Savannah repeated what she'd said as Justine sat there, unable to speak while Savannah begged her to say something.

"Does he know?"

"Does who know?" Savannah asked.

"Why your special gentleman friend from France, of course." Justine winked. "I've known you a long time, Savannah, and you're not one to sleep around so logically he could be the only one."

Savannah told Justine of her trip, and all that had transpired. She spoke of Larson, and how incredible he is, and of Caroline, and how awful she'd treated her. Savannah was an hour into the story before she realized the time, and they needed to get back to work.

"So what will you do?" asked Justine.

Savannah shrugged her shoulders as she got up to head back to work. It was quiet in the car until Justine asked her if she had decided what she would do about her pregnancy, telling her she had options.

"What do you mean? I could never..." she said, with tears streaming down her face.

"Please don't cry, we'll figure this out, but eventually people are going to notice. I thought you were gaining a little weight."

"Have you told your mom and dad?"

"I will tell them, just not now, Justine." They pulled up to the office, and Justine suggested, she go to the bathroom, and put some cold water on her face before returning to her desk.

"Savannah, don't worry I'll come over tonight, and we can talk." Savannah shook her head as she entered the bathroom.

* * *

Larson had just finished getting dressed when Charles knocked on the door.

"Good evening, Mr. Mansfield, your mother, and the lovely Ms. Lisette are waiting in the car."

"Great," said Larson, "let's get this night over with."

"Pardon me, Mr. Mansfield. I don't mean to speak out of place, but you don't seem to be interested in dinner tonight."

Larson grinned. "Don't mind me, Charles. I have other things on my mind."

"Like Ms. Savannah, sir."

Larson smiled. "Yes, like Ms. Savannah."

Charles opened the door, and Larson got in next to his mother.

"I'm not known to bite," said Lisette, "but you do look good enough to taste.

Caroline raised her brow.

She looked stunning in a red sequence dress with a slit up to her upper thigh. Larson couldn't help but

95

notice how beautiful Lisette was, but that had never been their problem. Lisette was selfish and cold; their problems went so much further than what you could see. They arrived at the restaurant and were immediately escorted to the best table with skyline views.

During dinner, Larson hardly spoke, prompting Caroline to say, "Lovely music tonight, Larson. Why don't you ask Lisette to dance?"

Larson glared at his mother as Lisette stood saying, "I'd love to."

Reluctantly he led her to the center of the floor, and they danced. Suddenly, he was no longer with Lisette, but rather dancing with Savannah. Larson pulled her closer thinking of the night he and Savannah had danced together. He could smell Savannah's perfume when Lisette said, "It's been a while since you've held me this close." Larson didn't say anything, he was still thinking of Savannah.

"Are you listening to me, Larson?"

"What?" He'd forgotten his arms were around Lisette.

"You seem preoccupied," said Lisette.

"I'm sorry; I have a lot on my mind with this trip."

"Maybe I can visit while you're there, and give you some company."

"That won't be necessary; I won't have time for anything but work." The band stopped playing, and

Larson returned Lisette to their table. Pulling out her chair he said, "Would you both, please excuse me," as he headed in the direction of the restrooms leaving his mother and Lisette staring after him.

"You two looked good out there together," said Caroline.

"I think so, but he seems as though his minds on something else."

Caroline looked at Lisette. "I think I may know what it is."

"Really. What then?"

Caroline told Lisette of the phone conversation between, Larson and Savannah.

"So you listened in on the conversation; you are a woman after my own heart."

Caroline nodded. "One of us may have underestimated the other."

"So what will you do, momma Caroline?" Lisette smirked.

"Don't you worry your pretty little head? I'll be taking care of my pest problem very soon?"

They clinked their glasses together, then began to drink.

Larson returned to the table. "So what are we toasting?"

"Why you, my dear, here's to a safe trip and an easy takeover."

"Thank you, Mother."

Caroline saw the suspicion in his expression, but she had no doubt he would come around.

Caroline made her best attempts at matchmaker, and Lisette fed the efforts by subtly bringing up their past relationship.

"Mother, I'm tired; I need some sleep."

"It's only 10:00 o'clock, Larson," Lisette said.

Caroline felt her annoyance with her son grow as he ignored his date.

After leaving the restaurant, they dropped off Lisette; Caroline wanted to spend some time with Larson before dropping him off for the night.

"Larson, dear, are you ready for the demanding week ahead of you?"

"Of course, Mother. How many times have we done this? I'd think by now you'd have more faith in me."

"I just don't want anything clouding your judgment."

"I'm fine, Mother no need to worry."

Even so, Caroline worried, not about the takeover, but the conversation she'd heard earlier.

"I may be going out of town for a few days while you're away," Caroline said.

"Really; where to?"

"Nowhere important, just something I let myself get talked into," she said. "Not to worry I won't be gone long, and you have my number if you need me."

Nine

Savannah arrived home to find Justine already waiting at the door. "You made it here fast."

"I didn't want to waste any time," said Justine.

They put their bags down, and Savannah asked if she'd like some tea. They both sat there looking at each other for a moment before Justine spoke.

"So you're having the baby, have you spoken to the father?"

Savannah looked at her with tears in her eyes saying, "I speak with him often."

Justine asked if Larson knew about the baby. How was she going to tell him and her parents? She hung her head and began to cry, she seemed to be doing a lot of that lately.

"You have to tell them," said Justine.

"I know. But what do I say? How can I tell him this news after only spending a few weeks with him?"

"He deserves to know, Savannah, and the longer you keep this from him, the more he may resent you for it."

Savannah knew Justine was right and whatever the outcome, she would have to provide for her child.

"So, tell me about Larson."

Savannah's cheeks heated.

"Well, it's obvious you care for him."

"I do. I think I'm in love with him."

Justine asked if she had told Larson how she felt and better yet, had he told her.

"I've wanted to," said Savannah. "But he's expressed feelings for me."

"What do you mean expressed feelings for you? Has he told you he loves you? It's either yes or no," pushed Justine.

"No, he hasn't said those exact words. There's something else I need to tell you about his mother, Caroline." Savannah told Justine what had happened between her, and Caroline. She explained the reason she'd returned home early.

"Savannah, I understand a mother being over protective of a son, but if you ask me, she's crossed the line. So what did Larson say about what happened?"

"He said 'those are her feelings, and words, not mine.' I know he spoke with her about it, he was furious."

"Well at the very least he stood up for you,"

Justine said. Just as she began to say something else, the phone rang.

"It's Larson," Savannah said as she answered the phone.

Justine smiled.

"Hello."

"Savannah, hi, how are you?"

"Much better. How was dinner?"

"Please, don't ask; it was a nightmare. I'll be leaving in the morning; I'll call you when I get settled into the hotel."

Justine waved her hands at Savannah, asking for the phone.

"Let me say hello, Savannah," shouted Justine.

Savannah motioned back no, with her hands.

"Savannah, is something wrong? You seem preoccupied."

"I'm sorry; I have company."

"Anyone I should be jealous of?" he asked, laughing.

Savannah smiled. "No, it's just my best friend Justine." She hit the speakerphone button.

"*Bonjour*, Larson," Justine shouted.

"Did she just speak French?"

"Cajun French."

"She speaks Cajun French?"

"We both do," said Savannah, "I thought I told you?"

Suddenly, Justine grabbed the phone, "*Comment allez vous*?"

"I'm fine, and you?"

Justine laughed and Savannah sighed.

"*Quel est votre nom*?" he asked.

"I'm Justine."

"*Mon nom est,* Larson,"

They both began to laugh, and before long Savannah joined them.

"So, you are a friend of Savannah?" Larson inquired.

"Only her best friend." Justine responded with a little attitude. "And I know all about you."

Larson laughed, saying, "Ahh, you two were talking about me?"

"Maybe," said Justine.

"So, why am I just hearing about you?"

Savannah reached out, and grabbed the phone just as Justine was about to say something. "I'm sorry, Larson that was my overly protective guard dog."

"I'm glad there's someone looking out for you, Savannah. I was just going to ask her if there were any guys hanging around there."

Savannah laughed. "Not one."

Justine motioned to Savannah that she would be heading home and at the same time yelled out, "Goodbye, Larson."

"Please tell Justine it's been a pleasure and good

night."

Justine let herself out, and Savannah and Larson continued to talk. She decided to ask him how he felt about the two of them, but kept beating around the bush.

"Savannah, what is it? Just tell me," asked Larson.

"Okay, here goes, where do you see this relationship going? We're thousands of miles from each other. We speak on the phone several nights a week, but how long will that be enough for you?"

"Savannah, I understand what you're asking, and I wish I had the answer, but honestly, I don't know."

She sighed, and he could tell she was getting frustrated. "Savannah, all I can tell you is that not a day goes by when I don't think about getting on a plane just so I can see your face, and hold you in my arms. The truth is, it's been hard, and I don't know how much longer we can do this, but I do know I need you in my life."

Emotions warred inside her and had her close to telling Larson about the pregnancy, but the decision to be with her had to be his, and not because she's having his baby.

"Savannah," said Larson, "never doubt my feelings for you. I could never forget about you. "

Savannah felt as though her heart would burst out of her chest. Before she knew it, the words rolled softly off the tip of her tongue. "I love you."

With no hesitation, she heard. "I love you too."

Right then she decided she would tell him, but not over the phone, not before his trip. She'd have to wait until he returned home. Before hanging up she said, "Larson, there is something I need to speak with you about."

"What is it?" he asked.

"This will take some time, so I'd rather wait until you get back, but don't worry it will hold."

"Are you sure?"

"I'm sure. Call me when you get in and have a safe trip."

As she hung up the phone, a sense of relief washed over her. She knew he loved her, and now there was no doubt she loved him.

She called her parents and invited them over for dinner the next night. The time had come to tell them the truth.

Getting ready for bed came easy, the sleeping part not as much. She lay there, eyes wide open, staring at the ceiling, waiting for tomorrow to come. No doubt she would disappoint her parents, especially her mom. She'd always dreamed of the day Savannah would get married and have children–in that order.

This would surely break her mother's heart.

She rolled over looking at the clock. 2:00 a.m. She had to get some sleep. She rolled over and closed her eyes.

Ten

Caroline looked at her watch. Larson should be boarding his flight for the four-hour trip. They were both anxious to turn around the company. She'd already worked out the details of her plans. She'd simply hire a private investigator to keep tabs on Savannah, and report back to her.

With everything in place, she would not have to leave France, and she would not have to lie to Larson about the trip; all she needed was the investigator. Normally, this would be work for her secretary, but she didn't want to take any chances on Larson finding out. She pulled up the Internet and did a search for private investigators in Carencro, Louisiana. Caroline knew where to look because she had already traced the number Larson had called from the office. Only a few numbers came up, so Caroline decided to check the town right outside Carencro, Lafayette. She picked one out and dialed.

"Cormier and Prejean Detective Agency; how can I help yah, *chere*?"

"I am in need of your services; I would like to hire you."

"Well, little lady, you called the right place. We run a top-notch facility here, my name is Prejean. My partner is Cormier. Who do I have the pleasure of talking to?"

Caroline swallowed a sound of disgust. "My name is unimportant, is that going to be a problem?"

"No problem here, as long as yah money is green like ours. I don't care what yah name is."

"Well," Caroline said, "here is what I need you to do."

"I'm making notes, *chere*."

"I need you to follow someone. I need her to be under scrutiny for the next seventy-two hours. I want every detail of her movements." Caroline paused. "Can you handle this?"

"Show nuff, little lady. You want pictures with the report."

"Don't call me little lady," Caroline said.

"Sorry, ma'am; I meant no disrespect, but I have to tell yah this job ain't gonna be cheap. We request money up front."

"Fine," said Caroline, "how much and where do I send it?"

"That'll be three thousand dollars, and you can wire it. Once the money is here, we'll start the job."

"What do you mean once the money's there?"

"We don't start until there's cash in hand," said Prejean.

"Fine, what if I give you another thousand and you to start now. I will have it wired to you by morning."

"Well, I think ya'll just got yah self a private investigator."

"Fine, I expect to hear from you at the end of each day."

She hung up the phone. "Imbecile!"

* * *

Savannah decided she would cook dinner for her parents before breaking the news to them. Justine had called early that morning to find out about Savannah's and Larson's conversation last night after she'd gone home. Justine was disappointed to hear Savannah hadn't told Larson about the baby, but glad she would finally be telling her parents. Savannah had everything prepared; crawfish etouffee, cornbread, collards, sweet tea, and cobbler for dessert, all of her parents' favorites.

Savannah set the table with the good china, given to her by her grandma who'd passed away two years earlier. The doorbell rang, startling Savannah. At that moment, she wished she could change her mind about telling them, but it was too late. She opened the door.

"Mom, Dad, I'm so glad you could come."

"We were a little surprised, but thanks for asking us," said Adele.

"Dinner's all ready and on the table if you'd like to wash up." Her mom and dad went to the restroom together. They didn't close the door all the way and she could hear them talking.

"Do you know what's going on?" asked Maurice.

"I'm sure I don't," her mother said. "Savannah has never cooked dinner like this. I expected spaghetti. Did you see? She had the good china out. You don't think something's wrong with her, do you? What if she's dying? What if it's that bug she caught?"

"Adele, calm down," said Maurice.

"Listen, Adele, there's no need to get hysterical. Let's just go have dinner, and if there's something wrong, I'm sure she'll tell us."

Savannah sighed. She had to tell them now. "Mom, Dad, everything all right in there?"

"Yes, dear, we'll be right out," said Adele.

They all sat down for dinner, each one looking at the other, until finally her dad asked, "Everything okay with you, Savannah?"

"I have something I need to tell you both, but I'm not quite sure how to say it."

"Just come on out with it, honey. We'll understand," Maurice said.

Adele suddenly started crying. "Oh, my poor

baby. Maurice something's wrong with her. What are we going to do?" Her mother became almost hysterical thinking the worst.

"Adele, calm down so she can finish," Maurice chimed in.

Savannah started again. "You both know I love you very much, and I never want to cause you any pain." Adele started crying again. Maurice held his wife, trying to comfort her when she shouted, "She's dying, my baby's dying."

Savannah's head began to spin. All of a sudden she shouted, "I'm not dying. I'm pregnant." All sound ceased, even the air seemed to stop. They stared at each other, waiting for someone to say something.

"Savannah, did you just say you're pregnant?" Adele asked.

"Yes, Mom, I'm pregnant."

"Thank God," said Maurice "at least she's not dying."

They all laughed heartily with such relief, all for different reasons. Then suddenly it went quiet again.

"Savannah," said her dad, "I'm going to take some of this food home with me to eat. I think you, and your mother needs to talk."

"Dad I need to explain this to you both."

"This is a mother-daughter talk. Your mom will fill me in when she gets home." Before walking out the door, her dad kissed her on the cheek saying, "Always remember I love you, and I'm here if you ever need me."

Both Savannah and her mother were too worked up to eat, so they got up from the table and went to the living room to talk.

"Mom, I'm so sorry for embarrassing you both."

Her mother took her hand and held it tightly. "Savannah, I thought you were dying, nothing puts things into perspective better than that. Just tell me who? We'll get through this together. You do know who, right?"

"Mother," Savannah said shocked. "It was my first time," she said, with tears in her eyes.

Savannah sat there for hours telling her mother about Larson, and her trip to France. She explained every vivid detail. They laughed, they cried, and they talked about the future.

Finally, her mom asked, "What are you and Larson's plans?"

Savannah looked at her mother, and the tears began their rapid descent.

"Savannah, did I say something wrong? Why are you upset? Is he not happy about the baby?" She looked into Savannah's eyes, and right away she knew. "Why haven't you told him?"

"I honestly don't know, I guess fear of what he might say, or just the fear of possible rejection."

"Savannah, he has a right to know, no matter what

the outcome, it's still his child." Her mom called home letting her dad know she would be staying the night. They had so much to talk about. She hung up the phone saying, "I'll make us some tea before we continue talking."

Savannah told her about Caroline. How she'd treated her the day she'd come to the chateau.

Her mother became enraged. "She may be rich, but that doesn't give her the right to treat you badly."

"That's why I ended my trip early; I didn't see any point in staying."

Adele asked Savannah if she'd told Larson about Caroline's treatment of her. Savannah confessed she hadn't told him until after she'd returned to the states.

"Savannah, I must ask you something very important, but I need you to think about it before you answer."

"What is it, Mom?"

"Do you love him?"

She took her mother's hand, sucked in a breath, and said, "With all that I am." Her mother always could tell when she was telling the truth just by looking in her eyes. It's the one thing that always gave Savannah away.

"And what of his feelings for you, has he spoken those words as well?"

"Yes, he has." Savannah smiled

"With sincerity?"

"With sincerity, Mom."

Morning had almost broke when they finally got ready for bed.

"Savannah, I want you to know that your father, and I love you. We will always be here for you no matter how this plays out."

"Thanks, Mom, I love you too." She kissed her forehead and turned out the light.

* * *

Larson finished getting settled into the hotel, and wanted something to eat before going to bed. He looked at the time and decided not to call Savannah. It was too early, and he didn't want to wake her. Instead, he called Caroline to let her know his flight had made it in. Undecided about what he ought to eat, he looked at the hotel menu, ordering in instead. As he laid there thinking about the last conversation he'd had with Savannah, he couldn't get her off his mind, and it made him laugh. Never had he felt this way, and it had gotten so far out of control the only thing he could do was smile.

* * *

Savannah woke smelling the aroma of her favorite coffee. "Thank you, Mom, I needed that." She reached for a cup then poured some for herself.

"Savannah, dear, I'm sorry, but I don't think you should be drinking caffeine until you've seen the doctor."

"The doctor. She jumped up. I almost forgot; I have an appointment at 10:00 o'clock today. "Calm down, Savannah." Her mom patted her hand. "It's only 7:00 o'clock. You have time."

Savannah fidgeted under her mother's touch.

"Savannah, would you like for me to go with you? I can call your father and let him know I'll be home later."

She looked at her mother, nodding. While her mother called her father, Savannah gathered her clothes and headed off for a hot shower.

Her father had brought clothes for her mother after she'd decided to stay overnight. While Savannah showered, she could hear her mother mumbling.

"My little girl has life inside her, a child who will change our lives forever." She began to softly, cry, and at that moment, Savannah stepped back into the bedroom to find her mother sitting on her bed.

"Mother, are you all right?"

She nodded.

"I'm so sorry I never meant to cause you pain," said Savannah.

"Pain, these aren't tears of sorrow." She took Savannah by the hand and pulled her close. "One day, after your child is born, you'll know what these tears are for. Believe me, when I tell you they are not tears of pain."

Shortly before 10:00 o'clock they headed out to

the doctor's office. It wasn't far from home, but the usual first visit paper work needed filling out. Savannah arrived in plenty of time at the office with her mother.

"Hello; may, I help you?"

"Yes, I have an appointment today with Dr. Martin."

"Name please?"

"Savannah Monreaux."

"Ms. Monreaux, please have a seat, and fill these out. The doctor will call you in momentarily."

Savannah and her mother sat and began filling out what seem like a novel of paperwork. Twenty minutes passed before Savannah heard her name. She stood, grabbing her mother's hand, pulling her into the office. "Dr. Martin will be in shortly," said the nurse. "Ms. Monreaux, I need you to remove your clothes, and put on this gown." After what felt like a lifetime the doctor walked into the room.

"Ms. Monreaux, hi, I'm Dr. Martin."

"Hello, Dr. Martin. I'm Savannah, and this is my mother Adele."

"Well, Ms. Monreaux, I see you were referred to me by Dr. Broussard. Looking over your chart you are a few months pregnant, but we will be running blood work and doing a sonogram today to make sure everything is starting out well." During the sonogram, the room was so still all you could hear was the sound

114

of the baby's heartbeat. "Well, Ms. Monreaux, you definitely have a passenger for the next few months, and everything points to a healthy baby so far."

"Thank you," said Savannah.

"Ms. Monreaux, from your chart I see this was not a planned pregnancy. Dr. Broussard tells me you've decided to keep your baby; I'm going to give you some information on resources for single parents. I take it the father is out of the picture."

"He doesn't know; I haven't told him yet."

"Ms. Monreaux, do you need to speak to someone. I know a great therapist who works with battered women."

"What," said Savannah. "No-no-no it's not like that at all. I plan to tell him, I just haven't done it yet."

"Okay, if there aren't any more questions, the front desk will make your next appointment, and congratulations, Ms. Monreaux."

Savannah stopped at the desk for the appointment and asked when she would get results from the test.

"We will call as soon as they come in don't worry," said the receptionist.

Savannah and her mother left the clinic. "Mom, is he very disappointed in me?"

"Is who disappointed, Savannah?"

"Dad, is he very disappointed?"

"Your father loves you very much and is trying his hardest to accept that his little girl is all grown up; just

115

give him some time."

Savannah drove her mother home after the appointment. She knew there was much to talk about with her dad, but the idea scared her. She stopped the car, but didn't get out.

"You will have to face your father someday," said Adele.

"I know, just not today." Her mother came around the car and gave her a kiss goodbye. "Try not to worry, Savannah, everything will be fine."

* * *

Larson's day had just gotten started and all indication led to it being long and exhausting. He'd attempted to call Savannah several times but, only reached her voicemail. Determined to get a hold of her, he dialed her number and finally, an answer.

"Hello," said a soft sweet voice.

"Savannah, hi it's Larson, I've been trying to reach you is everything all right?"

"Everything is fine."

"You sound tired; are you sure you're well?"

"I'm sure; it's just been a hectic few days. How are things going with the company change over?"

"Everything is going well, I should be home within a week at this rate." Savannah knew the time had come to tell Larson the news, but this was not something you just blurt out over the phone. "Larson, I think we need to talk but, I think it needs to be in person."

"What's wrong; are you sure you're okay?" Larson tried not to sound desperate.

"Yes, but we really do need to talk."

"Savannah, if you're going to break my heart I think I'd rather you do it while I'm thousands of miles away."

Savannah giggled. "I promise it's not at all what you're thinking, but it is important."

"Alright, I can schedule a flight out as soon as I'm done here at the end of the week. Is that okay?"

"That will be perfect."

Larson liked that she sounded excited about seeing him again. "I'll set everything up, Savannah, and let you know when to expect me. I'd better go; I'll call you later."

* * *

Caroline picked up the phone. After a brief greeting, she listened.

"Miz Mansfield, we're downloading the pictures and notes just like you wanted; you should have them shortly."

"Great," Caroline said. "I'm anxious to see what she has been upped to. I still have two more days of surveillance; so stay close to her."

"Don't you worry, I'm on her like a tick on a dog," said Cormier.

Moments later, Caroline got the files and began to

117

view them.

"What's this?" said Caroline. "Who is the woman with her? Well, this doesn't help, so she's going into a building that tells me nothing. What is she doing there?" *Why would you take the picture, and not tell me where she is?* She got on the phone and called Prejean.

"Cormier and Prejean, how can I help you?"

"This is Caroline Mansfield, you idiot."

"Well, no need for the name calling; what's the problem, *chere*?"

"The *problem* is your surveillance footage."

"What do you mean?" said Prejean.

"How am I supposed to know where she's going if you don't write it in the report or take a picture of the name?"

"Hold on there, *chere*, did you look at the second download?"

"What?" Caroline said.

"There's more than one file with pictures in it. You might want to continue looking. I think you'll be pleased with what you find."

Caroline hung up the phone without even a goodbye and continued looking at the second set of pictures.

Caroline was clicking through more images when she saw one of Savannah and the other woman leaving an office building. "Okay, so she's leaving an *OBGYN*

118

office. There has to be some kind of explanation; it must be that one time of the year all women dread." *That has to be it? What else could it be?* Caroline had dialed Cormier and Prejean's before she finished viewing the rest of the pictures.

"Private investigation, how can I help you?"

"This is Caroline Mansfield; I need you to keep a close watch on Ms. Monreaux. Let me know as soon as she goes back to the *OBGYN office.*"

"Sure thing, Miz Mansfield I'm on it," said Cormier.

Caroline hung up the phone and began shouting for Charles.

"Yes, Mrs. Mansfield, you called."

"Bring the car around; I have a few errands I need to run."

She picked up the phone and called Lisette.

"Hello, Lisette speaking."

"We need to talk. Meet me at the Carrousel du Louvre shopping mall in twenty minutes."

"Caroline, I'm in the middle of getting my nails finished; can't this wait."

"Twenty minutes; I'll see you there," said Caroline.

Eleven

"So have you told Larson yet?" asked Justine. Savannah had met her friend for lunch and was finally feeling like her day was heading somewhere.

"No, but I did tell him we needed to talk, and he'll be coming to Louisiana at the end of this week."

"Savannah, I am so proud of you," said Justine.

"I'm scared. What if this isn't something he's ready for."

"Listen, ready or not, you have to tell him, and let the chips fall where they may. Whatever happens, you have a family, and friends who love you. No worries, okay."

She smiled back at Justine. "I know you're right; everything will be fine."

The next day after work her mom decided to surprise her with a shopping spree for maternity clothes and things she would need once the baby comes. "Savannah, your father and I have decided we will be helping you out with things for the baby."

"Mom, I can't let you do that. The baby is my responsibility."

"Savannah, we are not asking permission. This is our only grandchild, and we are intent on spoiling him, or her, to our delight." She smiled at her mother. "This baby is going to be very fortunate to have grandparents like you and Dad."

They spent the day bustling in and out of baby stores, buying anything unisex since they didn't know if the baby would be a girl or boy.

* * *

Caroline sat across from Lisette waiting for her response to the news.

"Are you telling me you think she's pregnant?" Lisette asked.

"No, I'm saying I don't know. There are many reasons she could be in that office and I intend to find out why."

"So if she is ..." but before Lisette could finish her words Caroline said in an unusually low tone, "don't even think that."

"Caroline, I know you're not particularly fond of the girl, but Larson obviously has feelings for her."

"What are you saying?" Caroline asked. "You act as if you want them together."

"That's not it, Caroline, but he is a grown man and

very capable of knowing what he wants."

"Is that concession I hear in your voice? The great Lisette is giving up so easily."

"Not by a long shot, although I do think there's a chance we'll bump into each other this week."

Caroline smiled. "Now there's the Lisette I know and love." They finished dinner, but Caroline didn't stay around to chat as she was eager to get home, hoping there would be more news from Prejean.

* * *

Savannah and her mom had just gotten back from shopping, and were looking at all the purchases they'd made.

"Mom, you spent too much; please let me pay for some of this."

"Savannah, this was your dad's idea, and it would break his heart if you didn't accept it."

"Dad wanted to do this?" she asked, surprised.

"Yes, Savannah, your father loves you very much. He's happy he's going to be a grandpa; he's already calling himself Paw Paw Maurice."

"Paw Paw Maurice, huh?" Savannah smiled.

The ring of the phone interrupted their laughter. Adele glanced over at Savannah and smiled.

"Larson, how are you doing?" Savannah asked, excited to hear his voice.

"Tired and busy, but I wanted to hear your voice. Are you busy?"

"Not really, my mom is here visiting."

"Oh, I'm sorry; I can try you later."

"No, it's okay I was hoping to introduce you two, so this works out great. Do you mind saying hello? We won't keep you long."

"No, not at all. I would love to meet your mother, even if it is over the phone."

Savannah pushed the speakerphone button then gave her mother the phone. "He wants to say hi.

"Hello," said Adele. "It's so nice to meet you."

"*Bonjour madame, comment allez-vous?*"

"Fine, and you?" replied Adele. "I see you know the family secret."

Savannah laughed. "I did tell him we speak the language."

"It is so nice to meet you, although I am sorry it has to be over the phone," said Larson.

"Well it's nice to put a voice with the name," said Adele.

"Someone's been talking about me?" He laughed.

"Let's just say I may have heard it once or twice." Adele laughed back. Savannah quickly grabbed the phone from her mother. "Okay, that's enough of that."

"What happened?" said Larson, "We were just getting to the good stuff."

"I'll bet you were." Savannah chuckled. "So tell me, are you eating? Because I know when you're busy with your work you somehow forget to eat."

"Don't worry; I'm eating, just not sleeping." They talked until Larson said he needed to go. "Savannah," he said in a whisper before hanging up, "I miss you, and I'm looking forward to seeing you soon."

"I miss you too," she said in a soft voice, so her mother couldn't hear her as she hung up the phone. Her mother stood staring at her.

"What?" said Savannah in an excited tone shrugging her shoulders?

"You're glowing," said Adele. "I can see why you love him."

"Is it that obvious?" Savannah questioned.

"Not to the rest of the world, but I'm your mother, trust me, it shows."

Savannah took her mother's hands in hers. "It's like nothing I've ever felt before."

"That's why they call it love," said Adele. "That's why they call it love."

* * *

Caroline sat at home with a drink in her hand. She'd had plenty at dinner, but it gave her something to do while she waited for Prejean's update. Once she received the report, she set down her glass to scan through the photos. When she came across the pictures of Savannah and the other woman coming out of an infant and toddler boutique she gasped.

"What's this?" she asked aloud, looking at the pictures. "This can't be! There has to be a mistake. She

124

must be purchasing those items for someone else. That *poubelle sud* is not going to ruin my son's life with this." Enraged, Caroline banged the mouse on her desk, screaming with such force it roused the rest of the house.

"Is everything all right, Mrs. Mansfield? Are you okay?"

When her servant came into the room, she sucked in several deep breaths and grabbed her glass.

"I'm fine, Charles. I'm sorry if I disturbed you. Please go back to bed."

"Well, if you're sure there isn't anything I can do for you, I will retire for the evening." By this time Caroline's head was spinning. "Charles," she said, stopping him before he had a chance to leave.

"Yes, Mrs. Mansfield."

"I will need you in the morning, Charles, to take me to the airport."

"Are you paying Mr. Mansfield a visit?" Charles asked.

"No, I'm going out of town for a few days. I'll have my bags ready in the morning."

"Yes, Ma'am, will you need anything more tonight?"

"No, thank you, Charles. I'll see you in the morning."

Caroline immediately called the airport for a flight out. Once again this was not something she'd normally do herself, but she wanted no one to know about her trip to Louisiana. The more she thought about it, the angrier she got. The angrier she got, the more she drank. By 1:00 a.m. she'd gotten so drunk she passed out. Despite that, she had her bags waiting by the door for Charles.

"Shall I pick you up at the airport on your return trip?" he asked.

"That won't be necessary, Charles. I will get a cab home."

"A cab, really, ma'am, it's no trouble at all. I could be waiting at the airport when you get in."

"Thank you, Charles, but I'll be fine."

Caroline's phone rang just as the car pulled away. When she saw Larson's number, she had a flash of panic.

Looking at the number, she answered. "Hello, son, how are you?"

"I'm fine, Mother, and you?"

"Oh, things are great. Is everything okay at the company?"

"I'll be wrapping up everything by Friday, and returning home."

Larson had not yet told Caroline of his plans for a short vacation or that he would be seeing Savannah.

"So where are you? It sounds as though you're in the car, Mother?"

"Yes, I am, son. I will be out for a day or two

handling business."

"Business? Is everything all right?" he asked.

"Yes, son, everything's fine, I'll see you by the end of the week."

"Have a safe trip, Mother. Call if you need anything."

The limousine arrived at the airport and Caroline waited as the porter gathered her bags.

"I can wait with you, Mrs. Mansfield, until your flight leaves, if you like."

"Nonsense, Charles, go on home, there's plenty to take care of until I return."

"Yes, ma'am; you have a safe flight, and we will see you soon."

Twelve

Caroline's flight was long and tiring. Still nursing a hangover from the night before, she spent most of the flight sleeping it off. Prejean and Cormier had already been notified not to send anymore downloads until they heard from her.

Once she arrived in New Orleans, she boarded her flight to Lafayette, complaining the whole time about the city, the airport, and anything else she could think of. The flight was quick and turbulent, a far cry from her private jets with first class standards. She grabbed a cab to the hotel Orion Gold, the best the city had to offer. While unpacking, she spoke aloud to herself. "I have no idea what Larson could be thinking. He could never be happy here, it's not of his breeding. This town is below his stature. He would never be satisfied here; it's so simple." Once settled in, she called Cormier and Prejean telling them she no longer needed their services.

"Well, ma'am, I don't mean to overstep my boundaries, but it seems to me you would need us more now that you're here than before."

"And why is that?" Caroline asked in a sarcastic tone.

"You're in a strange city where you've never been before with people you don't know, trust me, you're gonna need our help."

She hated to admit it, but Prejean was right.

"Fine," she said with an attitude. "How much will this cost me?"

"That, *chere*, will depend on what you need."

"Look," Caroline shouted, "just meet me at my hotel tomorrow and get me to her home. I'll take it from there."

"Will do, but that will be five hundred dollars so we'll just keep your tab open in case you need us again."

She slammed the phone down. "Leeches, they're nothing but leeches." Caroline went out to find something to eat, settling for whatever she could get in the hotel restaurant. She returned to the hotel, exhausted, she went to bed going right to sleep.

* * *

Savannah awoke early and got ready for her workday. Her days seemed so much better now that the morning sickness had passed.

Work was hectic as usual. She'd been feeling more tired these days, not to mention her appetite had grown.

Justine popped her head into Savannah's doorway. "I have doughnuts, you want some?"

"You, my friend, are a lifesaver. I'm always hungry it seems."

"Well, you are eating for two," said Justine.

"I finally went down to personnel, and told them the news so I could find out about the insurance."

"How did it go, with Mrs. Wilson?" Justine asked.

"Well, you know Mrs. Wilson. She's like, 'Oh! Congratulations I didn't know you'd gotten married'."

Justine glared at Savannah. "Now you know she knew you were not married."

"I know, but I played along, and told her what she wanted to hear, I wasn't married."

"I would have told her to mind her own business, she is so nosey," said Justine.

"You got that right," said Savannah. "At any rate; I figure I won't have to tell anyone else, because by now I'm sure everyone knows." They both started laughing just as their boss passed by them.

"Okay, what's so funny?" he asked.

"Nothing," said Justine as she scurried out the door.

"Alright, Savannah, what's so funny?" asked her boss Mr. Leblanc.

130

"Honestly, nothing."

"I hear congratulations are in order for you."

"Thank you, sir."

"Please don't hesitate to tell me if you need anything we're all here for you."

"Thank you," she said, but she knew Mrs. Wilson had spread the word she was unmarried and pregnant.

As five o'clock rolled around, Savannah looked forward to going home. Before she could get out the door, her phone rang.

"Hello, Ms. Monreaux, this is Dr. Broussard. I have the result of your test available, and everything looks great. I'd like you to try and gain a little weight over the next few months, due to all the problems you had with morning sickness, you're a bit underweight."

A flash of panic surged through Savannah. "Is my baby all right?"

"Your baby is fine; I just want you to gain a little."

"I don't think that will be a problem. I recently started eating everything in sight."

"Great, then we won't have a problem with the weight next time I see you. I'd like to see you in a month so. Please call the front desk to make an appointment."

"I will; thank you so much."

Savannah got in her car and headed toward her mother and father's house. She'd promised to stop by and visit after work. Driving off, she noticed a car following close behind. She thought nothing of it until the car followed her into her parent's subdivision. She pulled into the drive as the car kept going.

They must live somewhere in the subdivision, Savannah thought. She went inside, staying longer than she planned. Her mother had cooked, and insisted she stay for supper.

* * *

Caroline parked down the road and turned the car around to make sure she wouldn't miss Savannah coming out. She sat there looking at the home, thinking. That must be her parent's home, obviously middle class, possibly even lower middle class. Caroline saw the door open, and three people stepped out. Savannah hugged her parents, said something, and left. Caroline had parked a street over and waited until she thought Savannah might be inside. She started the car, and drove around the block; as she drove by Savannah's car her phone rang causing her to jump.

She looked at the name, Larson Mansfield. She parked the car, turned off the lights, and said hello.

"Mother, how are things going with the trip?"

"Things are great. How are you?"

Larson told his mother how tired he'd been, but he should be home on Sunday. He wanted Caroline to have dinner with him on Sunday. She agreed. "Sunday, yes that would be fine. Listen, I'm busy right now, so I will have to talk to you later, Larson."

"Alright, I'll meet you Sunday at home I'll get a cab from the airport."

"Nonsense," said Caroline. "I'll have Charles pick you up; just let me know what time your flight arrives."

"Thank you," he said, "that would be great. I'll call you with the details."

Caroline knew she didn't have much time to find out more about Savannah, and that she had to be home before Larson on Sunday.

Just as, Caroline was about to leave for the hotel, she noticed someone leaving the apartment. Well, well, well what's this, Savannah going to throw the trash in a tight tee and stretch pants? Caroline stared, trying to see if Savannah's stomach had grown any since she'd seen her, but it was too dark to tell. Maybe she'd gone shopping for someone else, and this was just a big mistake. Maybe she isn't pregnant thought Caroline.

Be that as it may, she needed to know for sure before heading back.

* * *

Larson called Savannah, and they talked for over an hour.

"I really am anxious to see you."

"That means a lot to me, Savannah. But right now, you need to get some rest."

"Goodnight, Larson."

"Goodnight."

Savannah awoke the next morning with the remnants of paranoia nudging at her mind. She spent far too much time looking in her rearview mirror, expecting to find someone following her.

When she got to work, she decided she was worrying about nothing. But something still didn't feel right.

During lunch, she told Justine about her weird feelings the night before, and they both laughed at how ridiculous it sounded.

"What did you think, Savannah, that his mom hired someone to follow you? Do you know how crazy that sounds?"

Savannah knew it sounded crazy, but then she remembered how cruel and hateful Caroline had been to her, and how the woman had warned her not to get on her bad side.

"Savannah, snap out of it," said Justine. "You're worrying about nothing."

"Your right, I've made this whole crazy mess up in my mind practically scaring myself to death."

Savannah left the office that afternoon without a care, until she noticed someone sitting in a car in the parking garage. She held her keys tightly in her hand, looking over her shoulder as she opened the door, locking it as soon as she got settled in the seat.

She started her car and hurried out of the garage. I know I'm not crazy, but I'm sure it's the same car. She put her Bluetooth on and called Justine.

"Hello, Justine speaking."

"Justine, its Savannah."

"What's wrong girl; you sound hysterical?"

"Do you remember me telling you about the car following me yesterday?"

"I thought we settled this," said Justine.

"So did I, but it was just in the parking garage. There was someone sitting in it, and now their following me. Justine, I'm scared, what should I do?"

"Maybe you should just go to the police department and tell them what's going on, Savannah."

"Tell them what, Justine? That I think a car is following me, they'll think I'm crazy. I'm going to head out to my mom and dads' and maybe stay there tonight."

"Are you going to tell them what's going on?" asked Justine.

"No, I don't want to worry them. They've had enough to think about lately."

"How long will it take you to get to their house?"

"About thirty minutes, less if I speed it up a bit."

"Savannah, the roads are wet, it's been raining, please be careful."

"I promise, I'll be careful."

"Please, call me when you get there, I'm worried about you; okay?"

"Don't worry, Justine, I'll call."

Savannah drove as carefully as she could, but each time she looked in her mirror and saw the headlights, she speeded up a little. She didn't worry too much as the road had few curves. Moments later, she rounded one of those bends in the road.

The headlights of an oncoming truck flashed in her eyes. In the moments before the beams blinded her, she watched the truck swerve into her lane. She jerked the steering wheel, trying to get out of the way, but her tires slipped and she screamed as her car made impact with the guardrail. Her heart raced as the car flipped into the air. Savannah tried to hold on as the car flipped over and over, finally landing with a horrible crash.

* * *

Caroline watched in horror as Savannah's car rolled down into the ravine. When had their trip become a game of cat and mouse? She swerved just in time, missing the guardrail herself. She slammed on her brakes and the car skidded to a stop. Panic pushed its way into her mind as she dug around in her bag for her cell phone. "911. What's your emergency?"

"Oh God, oh God, she's hurt. Please send help quickly."

"Okay, ma'am, I need you to calm down, and tell me where you're at?"

"I don't know where I am. Help, please help, they're hurt."

"I'm sorry, how many people did you say are hurt?"

"I don't know; at least two," said Caroline.

Caroline noticed a man standing by the broken guardrail. The headlights from her car shone on him, making the blood on his face glisten. He wavered on his feet, looking disoriented.

"She looks hurt real bad, I'm going to try to get down there," he said.

"Just tell them where we are." Caroline shouted, "I don't know where we are, I'm not from here."

She handed him the phone. "Please talk to her. I don't know where we are."

He grabbed the phone giving their location then scurried down to help Savannah.

The panic in Caroline intensified. "What if they blame me for this? What if I'm responsible? *Larson will never speak to me again, I will lose my son*. She heard sirens in the distance. "No one knows my name or who I am."

"Oh God, I pray she's all right, But I can't let them find me here. I can't go to jail." She ran to her car, and drove off, having no idea where she was going.

She drove past the emergency vehicles as they rushed to the scene. She looked down into the ravine as she drove past. The car was totally crushed and no matter how much she prayed she feared there was no way Savannah could have survived.

* * *

Caroline made it back to her hotel room and was still shaking. "What did I do? I never wanted this to happen." She paced around her hotel room, wringing her hands.

She called the airport, trying to get a flight out; even if it were the red eye she knew she needed to leave. She was worried about Savannah, but no one could ever find out she'd been here. She called Cormier and Prejean

"I will no longer need your services. You are to destroy every trace of knowing me and never speak to anyone of our association."

* * *

Finally, after forty-five grueling minutes, the rescue worker pried the top off the car, allowing them to see Savannah. She lay in a pool of blood, wedged between the steering column and the front seat. The paramedic gently took her tiny wrist and felt for a pulse. She didn't respond, but her chest continued to rise and fall. They had no time to waste.

Officer Hebert watched as they loaded her onto the Med flight chopper to airlift her to the best trauma center in Lafayette. The officer retrieved her purse from the car and looked through it to find someone they could contact. He found her phone in her purse. He checked the call record and realized she'd been talking with someone not long before the accident. He

138

called the number, hoping to contact someone who may know her.

"Savannah, you had me worried. Where are you?"

"Hello, ma'am, I'm Officer Hebert. Are you a friend of the owner of this cell phone?"

"Yes, my name is Justine. Why are you calling from her phone? Where is Savannah?"

"Justine, do you know how to reach her next of kin?"

"Yes, I know her parents, what's wrong?"

"Ms. Monreaux has been in an accident; she's being airlifted to Saint Agnes Hospital. We need the family to meet them there."

"Oh my God."

"Ma'am, do you have a phone number and address where they can be reached?"

He listened.

"Did you say 1521 Pier road? That's just down the street; I'll head there now and break the news. I suggest you make it over to the hospital as soon as possible."

Officer Hebert pulled up to the house with lights flashing and siren on. Maurice and Adele met Officer Hebert at the door.

"Mr. and Mrs. Monreaux."

"Yes," the woman answered. "How may I help you?"

Officer Hebert looked at their faces and wondered how he was going to tell them they might lose their

139

daughter. "I'm so sorry, but there has been an accident involving your daughter."

"You must have the wrong house, you're mistaken. Our daughter is at home, she probably just got in from work."

"No, ma'am, there's no mistake. Your daughter is Savannah Monreaux, right?"

The husband caught his wife just before she hit the floor. She looked pale with all the blood drained from her face. "This can't be," she said, "is she going to be all right?"

"I'm here to take you to the hospital, her condition at this time is unknown, but time is of the essence."

* * *

Maurice and Adele grabbed their things and ran out the door, both stunned by the news. Adele cried uncontrollably, and her husband looked as if he had just been hit by a bus.

They arrived at the hospital where Justine waited.

"Justine, have you seen her? Is she okay?" Adele asked.

"They won't tell me anything, except they're working on her."

Adele went to the desk. "Please, miss, can you tell me anything about my daughter?"

"Name?" mumbled the receptionist.

"Savannah Monreaux."

"Please have a seat. The doctor will be out to

speak with you shortly." Maurice began pacing, Adele began crying again, and Justine tried to comfort them.

Minutes crept by like hours, but still there was no news.

Eventually, the doctor came out and called for the Monreaux family.

They gathered around, waiting. "Are you the parents of Ms. Monreaux?"

Adele couldn't respond, so Maurice chimed in. "Yes, doctor we are. How is our daughter?"

"We're still doing everything we can for your daughter. She has internal bleeding, and several broken bones; but more pressing is the swelling on her brain that's keeping her in a coma."

"Oh my," Adele shouted, "what about the baby?"

The doctor looked at her puzzled. "What baby? Is she pregnant?"

"Yes, almost six months along; didn't you know that?"

"We are still waiting for some results from the lab. I will inform you the moment we have more information. I need to advise my team of her pregnancy. Do you know who her OBGYN is? We will need to work together closely if they are going to survive. Prepare yourselves for a long night."

"This is a dream," said Adele, "A nightmare. Any minute I'll wake, and everything will be all right."

Maurice hugged her saying, "All we can do now is

pray."

Adele looked around the waiting room. Justine had contacted their employer, and by four in the morning the lobby had filled with friends and coworkers. Some slept while others talked, unable to fall asleep.

Savannah's doctor made his way down the hallway, followed by two more doctors.

Adele, Maurice, and Justine stood as the doctor asked could they speak in private. Justine turned, heading back to her seat.

"What are you doing?" Adele asked.

"I think he only wants the family."

Adele took one hand, Maurice the other. "You are family," they said as they entered the room, closing the door behind them. The lobby was still, not a sound from anyone as they waited to hear about Savannah.

Sometime later, Adele and Maurice, headed toward the chapel to light candles for their daughter, as Justine explained Savannahs condition.

"She's in a coma, and there's swelling to the brain. Right now they're trying to keep the swelling down, so they don't have to operate. She has multiple broken bones, and lacerations. They won't know if there is any paralysis until the swelling starts to go down. There is a ray of light under all this darkness. The baby is alive. Please keep Savannah in your prayers; she has a long, hard fight ahead of her."

Thirteen

Larson's week was finally reaching its end, and he was all too ready to head home. The thought of being able to spend time with Savannah had made the week so much easier to bear. He'd tried calling her earlier, but got no response. He tried again with no success. "It's getting late," he muttered. "I'll try her tomorrow; she's probably with her parents having dinner."

Over the next few days, Larson stayed busy finishing out the week. He still had not reached Savannah which had begun to worry him, but he figured they were just missing each other. His flight would be leaving soon so he called the front desk for a cab and prepared to head home.

* * *

Savannah's condition remained the same, and the doctors continued working hard to keep both Savannah and her baby alive. Adele and Justine had stayed at the hospital, neither of them having slept much that night.

Adele gazed over at her husband. He looked as though he hadn't closed his eyes for a minute. He looked up at her.

"How are you doing, Adele?"

"Better than you from the looks of things."

"How are you holding up, Justine?" he asked.

She shrugged her shoulders. They all sat waiting to be allowed to see Savannah for the first time; they would only have ten minutes. Adele clung to Maurice for support, so afraid of what she might see.

The nurse called for the Monreaux family, stating two visitors only. Justine looked at Adele, motioning for her and Maurice to go see their daughter.

"Nurse," said Adele. "Please would you allow three just this once?"

"I'm sorry, but hospital rules," she said.

Adele took Justine's hand. "This is the only person my daughter has ever known as a sister. Please, please, don't deny her the chance to see her."

The nurse looked at the three of them and then motioned them to follow. "You have only ten minutes. If you need us for anything, we'll be right outside the door."

Maurice squeezed Adele's hand, and they walked into the room. Savannah lay in the bed, bruised and bandaged; she appeared as though she was sleeping.

Adele led Maurice to one side of the bed, Justine

went to the other. They held her hands, trying desperately to hold in their grief. Adele had no idea if her daughter could hear them. "Savannah, this is your mom, sweetie, don't worry you and the baby are going to be just fine." Her voice cracked.

Maurice reached over, giving her a kiss on the only spot of her forehead not bandaged or bruised. "Baby, this is your dad; you keep fighting because that little one you're carrying needs your strength."

Justine squeezed Savannah's hand as she leaned in. "Fight, Savannah, fight with all your might to come back to us."

What seemed like two minutes had turned into ten, and it was time for them to leave the room. Walking out, Adele turned around and whispered, "You have to get better; you have to tell Larson he's a father."

A nurse met them in the hall. "The doctor would like to speak to you before you leave."

They all waited on pins and needles for the doctor to arrive. "Mr. And Mrs. Monreaux, I want to fill you in on how Savannah's night went. She is exceptionally strong. The good news is, her condition has not changed from last night, which means it hasn't gotten worse. We performed a sonogram, and the baby seems to be doing well.

"We won't know if there are any neurological issues with the baby until after the birth. For now, all we can do is sit and wait, but every day she stays in

145

stable condition, the better her chances, as well as those of the baby."

"That's good," Adele said.

"What I want the both of you to do is go home and get some rest. If there is any change, we will call."

"We can't leave her here alone; what if she needs us?" said Adele.

"Mrs. Monreaux, she is monitored twenty-four hours a day. I promise, she is in the best care. I need you and your husband to be well rested when she does come to. Now please, get some sleep."

Maurice took Adele by the hand. "He's right, honey. We're both exhausted, and Savannah will need us when she wakes. Justine," said Maurice, "I'll drop you off as well you need to get some rest. They all agreed as they left for home."

* * *

Larson's plane landed, and he spotted Charles who had come to pick him up from the airport.

"Welcome home, Mr. Mansfield."

"Thank you, Charles, how has everything been while I was away?"

"Quiet, sir."

"Mother hasn't been running you ragged, has she?"

"No, sir, she's been out of town, so it's been quiet."

On the ride home, Larson tried Savannah's phone again hoping he'd reach her; still no answer. He was beginning to worry. He'd been calling both her home and cell phone and getting the recorded message from both. They arrived at the mansion, and Larson went looking for Caroline. He found her in the study pacing back and forth.

"Mother, I thought after a week away, I might have gotten a better reception." She turned to Larson to say something, but the words would not come.

"My mother at a loss for words, are you feeling okay?"

"I'm fine, just happy to see you." She walked to him, put her arms around him, and squeezed tight. "I'm so glad you're home. How did everything go?"

"Well I have no doubt that this company will flourish and prove to be a formidable asset."

Larson watched as his mother stared off into space, uncharacteristically quiet.

"So, Mother, tell me about your trip?"

She started. "Nothing to tell, it was just a dull seminar I let Lisette talk me into."

After dinner, Larson went out to the terrace and tried to call Savannah once more. When he walked back in his mother looked noticeably worried. He ignored her.

"Is everything all right, son?" she asked with concern in her voice.

"Why do you ask, Mother?"

"You seem preoccupied, that's all. Is there anything I can do to help?" Larson was worried,

Savannah and he had made plans for him to visit and he had been unable to reach her. It wasn't like her not to call or at least leave a message. Larson waved her off when Caroline asked if he'd like to have a drink with her. "Thank you, Mother, but I'm tired and I just need to get some rest."

"Your father would be so proud of you," Caroline said with a smile on her face.

"That means a lot to me, Mother. I often wonder what he'd think of me."

"He would think you are a wonderful son, just as I do."

Larson walked out wondering what that was all about. Though he'd always assumed she was proud of him, she never said the words.

"Why don't you take some time off, Larson? After the week, you've had you deserve it. We can handle the office without you?"

Relief washed over Larson. Now he wouldn't have to tell Caroline anything about going visit Savannah.

"Larson, is there any place in particular you're interested in going?"

"No, I'm just looking forward to some time away from the office."

"Great, maybe we can have lunch during the week."

"Sure, Mother, I'll let you know what day," he said walking out the door.

Each day that passed had Adele and Maurice visiting their daughter at the hospital.

"She looks better, don't you think?" said Adele.

"Yes," said Maurice, "she's getting color back in her cheeks."

"Thank you, I needed to hear that."

"She's strong, Adele. We'll get through this; I promise."

"Maurice, can we go by Savannah's place on the way home, I'd like to pick up some things for her so it will feel more like home in the hospital? It's always cold in there, and she loves that throw her grandmother made for her one Christmas."

"Sure, dear, we'll drop by and pick it up I think she'd like that."

* * *

Larson couldn't sleep; he'd been staring at the clock most of the night when he decided to give it one more try, and call Savannah.

The phone rang, but this time instead of the machine, a voice said, "Hello."

"Savannah! Thank God, I've been trying to call you for days. Is everything all right?"

"I'm sorry," said Adele, "this is her mother."

"Mrs. Monreaux, it's Larson. I'm sorry to have called so late, but I've been trying to reach Savannah, is she available."

149

Adele began to cry as she handed the phone over to Maurice.

"Hello, this is Savannah's father, Please excuse my wife."

"Mr. Monreaux, I've been trying to reach Savannah."

"I'm sorry, son, but Savannah has been in a car accident."

"What did you say?" muttered Larson. He was sure he'd misunderstood.

"Savannah's in the hospital, in serious condition."

"I must have fallen asleep, and I'm dreaming. Yeah that's it, I'm dreaming, I'll wake up any minute now." Suddenly he heard Maurice's voice.

"Hello, are you there? Are you still there?"

"This can't be happening," said Larson with tears in his eyes.

"Would you happen to be Larson Mansfield?"

"Yes, I am. Is she all right?"

"You may want to get here as soon as possible. She's in a coma, and there has been no change since the accident." Larson wrote down the numbers Maurice gave him, thankful that someone would pick him up at the airport.

"Thank you so much," said Larson, "I will call you as soon as I get a flight out." Larson had not yet unpacked his bags from the week before so all he needed was a flight to the states. He considered calling

150

Caroline, but decided to wait, getting to Savannah had to be his first priority. Within thirty, minutes, he was at the airport waiting on the redeye. He boarded his flight and settled in for the long journey ahead.

As much as he needed the sleep, his mind kept racing back to Savannah, and what could have happened. What if I lose her, he thought. I don't think my heart could bear it. He closed his eyes in an attempt to sleep.

Fourteen

Larson arrived the next day, and Maurice and Adele stood waiting to pick him up. Adele knew Larson the moment she saw him. He looked just as Savannah had described. She wouldn't need the sign they'd made with his name on it.

"Hello, I'm Larson, are you Savannah's parents?"

"Yes, I'm Maurice, and this is my wife Adele."

Adele looked at Larson. "I can see the attraction my daughter has with you. Savannah mentioned you were handsome."

"Thank you," Larson lowered his head. "Your daughter is an amazing and beautiful woman."

Adele's eyes teared up as Larson reached down and hugged her.

"We need to go," Maurice said, grabbing one of the bags for Larson.

"Maybe you could help me out, Mr. Monreaux. I

didn't have time to get a hotel, and hoped you might know of one close by the hospital."

"Nonsense," said Adele, "we have room in our home, you're welcome to stay with us if you like."

"Are you sure it won't be any trouble?"

"Not at all," said Adele. "Besides, we have much to talk about involving our daughter. Mr. Mansfield would you like to freshen up before going to the hospital."

"Please, call me Larson, and if it's all right with you both, I'd really like to see Savannah."

"Sure," she said, "but I must tell you, she is very badly bruised with many broken bones."

Adele could see the pain in Larson's eyes; you could see his heart was hurting for Savannah. They arrived at the hospital, and took the elevator to Savannah's floor.

Adele opened the door and nudged Larson into the room. They all watched for a moment as Justine fluffed Savannah's pillow while humming a song. She didn't seem surprised when they walked in.

"Hello, my name is Justine; we spoke over the phone once."

"*Bonjour*, Miss Justine. I remember you well; sorry we have to meet under such circumstances."

* * *

Justine moved aside. Larson's heart nearly stopped when he saw Savannah.

She lay perfectly still with bandages covering her from head to toes, with tubes everywhere. He took her hand, bowed his head, and began to cry. "Savannah, if you can hear me, it's Larson. I'm here, and I promise I won't leave."

He watched Adele and Maurice kiss their daughter while taking Justine by the waist. "We'll give you some privacy," whispered Adele.

Larson nodded as they left the room. He sat looking at her, and in that one moment realized, he'd be lost without her. "Savannah, I know you can hear me. You must fight to come back to me, to all who love you." She looked so fragile, he had never seen her so vulnerable before.

* * *

Adele and Justine had settled in the waiting area "Adele, did you tell him? Does Larson know?"

"No, he doesn't know. We'll break the news to him tonight," she said.

"Savannah was right, he has to be the most handsome and dignified man I've ever met."

"I can see why she feels for him," said Adele.

Maurice chimed in, saying, "He's the lucky one. My little girl is beautiful inside and out." For the first time in days they all laughed. It felt good to Justine, and they needed to stay positive for Savannah. Larson had been in the room for nearly an hour, and Justine and Adele were starting to worry. They decided to

154

check on him. Adele opened the door. They found Larson had fallen asleep holding Savannah's hand with his head on the bed.

"Larson," said Adele, "we're going to visit for a moment, and then we'll take you home. Why don't you and Justine meet us in the waiting area."

"I'm sorry. One minute I was talking to her, and I guess I fell asleep."

"Go ahead, we'll be out shortly." He kissed Savannah softly on the cheek and whispered, "I love you," in her ear.

"Come on, Larson, let's sit."

Justine didn't miss the weary expression on his face.

"She's strong." said Justine, "if anybody can come through this, it's Savannah."

"I pray you're right. Because I don't know what I'd do without her."

"So you love her?" asked Justine abruptly.

"Yes, I do," he said in a soft voice.

They sat together talking about the trip, and how he and Savannah happened to get together. They talked about the trouble with Caroline, and how at some point he would have to face his mother, no matter the consequences.

Adele and Maurice met them in the waiting room after saying goodnight to their daughter.

"It's been a long night," said Maurice, "we should

head home."

"Justine, please give us a call when you get in, so we don't worry," Adele said.

"I will."

* * *

No one said a word on the car ride home, all three deep in their own thoughts, for different reasons. Approaching the house, Adele remembered what Savannah had told her about the Mansfield's house, and how beautiful it was. "I'm sorry," she said, "if the accommodations are not what you're used to, but its home."

Larson looked up to see a small brick house with a well-kept yard.

"This is perfect; it seems very peaceful and quiet. How long have you lived here?"

"Since Savannah was born," Maurice chimed in. "We bought this house while her mother was pregnant." They parked, got the bags, and went inside.

Larson could not hide his surprise as they entered the house. He stood for a moment, just looking around.

"We took a lot of pictures as she grew up. We knew she would be our only child," said Adele, giving him a warm smile.

"Why? Was there a problem having her?" Larson asked.

"Not at all," Adele replied, "we just weren't financially able to care for more than one child, so we put all we had into her." Larson, who had been born to privilege, tried to comprehend the selflessness of what Maurice and Adele had done. Because they knew they were unable to provide for more than one child, they made a sacrifice not to have more.

"I hope I'm not being too forward by asking this, but did you want more children?"

"We would have had a house full if we could have supported them all," said Adele.

Larson sat wondering why he had been so fortunate, and how he had taken things for granted until today.

Adele showed Larson to his room so he could unpack and take a shower. While getting towels together for Larson, Adele asked would he join them for a cup of coffee when he was finished.

"Normally, I don't drink coffee this late, but I could use a cup."

Adele turned, looked into his eyes, and said, "Believe me, you'll need it. We seriously need to talk, and it may take a while."

As Adele turned and walked away, Larson wondered what she'd meant. Was there something more to Savannah's injuries they hadn't told him?

* * *

Adele had made sandwiches, and a few snacks in case anyone got hungry. She sat the tray down and began to speak. First, she wanted to get to know more

157

about the man who had stolen her daughter's heart. They sat talking hours. He obviously loved Savannah, but was he ready to be a father.

"Larson, there is something we need to tell you. This is not the easiest thing to say, but you have a right to know. There is a reason Savannah wanted you here in Louisiana."

"Yes, ma'am, I know. We missed each other terribly."

Maurice spoke up. "While that is true, there's another reason she wanted you here."

"She didn't know how to tell you, and she didn't want to say it in a phone conversation," Adele said. "Upon Savannah's return home from France, she became ill."

"Yes," said Larson. "She'd gotten a terrible bug from work that was going around."

"That's what she thought, what we all thought. We were all mistaken."

"Then what did she have?" he asked, a look of panic in his eyes.

"The doctor ran some blood work." Adele hesitated for a moment then blurted out. "She's pregnant. You're going to be a father." Suddenly all the blood drained from his face.

"I'm what?" he said, now wearing a perplexed expression.

"Savannah is pregnant, that's what she wanted to

tell you before the accident."

"You said I'm going to be a father? Does that mean the baby is all right?"

"What we know right now is the baby appears to be fine, she's six months along." Larson's hands shook and he gasped for air. He stuttered out a few indistinguishable words, and then started to cry

Adele took him by the hand and tried to comfort him, but he was so shook up he could barely speak. "I'm going to be a father," he kept repeating aloud, then he became very still, almost as if in shock.

"Larson, are you okay?" asked Adele.

"Okay? No, not by a long shot."

Maurice stood, and began to speak. "Larson, I need to know where things stand between you and our daughter. Regardless of how things turn out, I need to know how you feel about Savannah."

Larson felt light headed, as though all the blood had rushed back into his head at once.

"Mr. Monreaux, from the moment I met your daughter I haven't been able to get her out of my mind. Coming here, and finding out I may never be with her again is more than my heart can bear. If that is not enough, I find out she is the mother of my child. With all my heart, I wish I could take her place. That it was me lying there in that hospital bed."

Adele watched the men; she could see the turmoil Larson was going through.

159

Maurice put his hand on Larson's shoulder. "I needed to know you are the right man for my little girl. There is no doubt to me that you are." Larson reached out his hand to Maurice to shake it. Suddenly, Maurice pulled him into a hug.

"Larson," said Adele, "I know we've given you a lot to think about tonight. Why don't you try to get some rest? Maybe you'll be able to process it better tomorrow."

He stood, said goodnight, and went to his room.

He sat on the edge of the bed and took off his shoes. Suddenly, he pulled his phone out of his pocket. Three missed calls. He'd turned off his phone at the hospital, and forgot to turn it back on. The calls were from Caroline, she had left messages asking him to call. He turned the phone back off; he had been through enough tonight. He would deal with his mother tomorrow.

That morning, Larson awoke thinking it had all been a dream until he saw Savannah's picture on the wall. He wanted to be at the hospital early. He hated leaving her last night, and didn't want her to be alone. Savannah's mom had made breakfast and insisted he sit and eat something. During breakfast, Larson got another call from his mother. Both Adele and Maurice noticed his unease about the call.

"Larson, if you need to get that, and leave the table it's all right," said Adele.

He took in a deep breath. "It's my mother, I haven't told her about Savannah, or that I'm here."

"Larson," said Adele, "we know about the situation between Savannah and your mother, but there is so much more at hand here. If you love my daughter as you say you do, you will do what's right by standing up to your mother."

Larson knew Adele was right it was time to stand up to Caroline regardless of the consequences. "I'll speak with her as soon as I check on Savannah," he told Adele.

"Larson, everything will work itself out don't you worry."

Larson knew his mother far too well, and he knew she would not take the news lying down.

"Would you like a ride to the hospital? We're going that way our self," said Maurice.

"Yes, thank you," said Larson.

As they passed the front desk on their way to Savannah's room, a nurse stopped them. Mr. and Mrs. Monreaux, the doctor would like a word with you both.

Adele began to panic. "Is she okay? Is my daughter all right?"

"There's been no change in your daughter's condition; the doctor will be with you shortly."

Dr. Vincent approached them with Dr. Martin, Savannah's OBGYN.

"Mr. and Mrs. Monreaux, would you please come

with me."

Adele took Larson by the hand introducing him as the baby's father. "Then you're going to need to come with us as well," said Dr. Vincent. He took them into a private room to speak. "I wish I had better news," he said, "but there has been a change in the baby's condition." The baby's heartbeat is too fast.

We have gotten back the results of a recent sonogram, and it shows the umbilical cord wrapped around the baby's neck."

Adele began to cry. "I can't lose my daughter, and my grandchild." Maurice put his arm around her and held her close to him.

"So what's our next move doctor?" Maurice asked.

"Normally, we would monitor the situation, making sure the cord doesn't get any tighter. The problem is Savannah has just made six months, and the baby is under-weight, in her condition we could lose them both."

"Larson looked at the doctor. What is it you need to save her life, money is no option. Do we need to fly in more surgeons? Just tell me, what do we need?"

Dr. Vincent turned to Larson saying, "You may, if you choose to, fly in other doctors, but I can assure you, we are the number one trauma center in the region, and we already have the best on staff."

"I'm sorry. I meant no disrespect. I'm only trying to save the life of the woman I love, and my child."

Adele took Larson by the hand, and Dr. Vincent continued. "As long as the cord doesn't get any tighter, we can continue to let the baby grow. But, if the cord continues to tighten, causing the air to the baby's brain to be cut off, it could cause permanent damage, even death."

"So what do we do?" Adele asked.

"We keep a close watch on her, and the baby, and pray there's no change with the umbilical cord," said Dr. Vincent.

They spent the day with Savannah, talking and praying she might hear them. Larson told about the baby and that he was there waiting for her to wake. He told her how excited he was that they were having a child together, hoping it would remove any doubt from her mind about his love for her.

Despite being emotionally exhausted, Larson stepped out to call Caroline. He had so much he needed to tell her, he had no idea where to start.

The phone rang, and he heard his mother's voice, "Caroline speaking."

"Mother, its Larson."

"Larson, where have you been? I've been calling for days; do you know how worried I am?"

"Mother, calm down. I need you to listen. I'm in Louisiana with, Savannah's parents."

Caroline didn't say anything.

"Savannah's been in a terrible accident; she's in a

coma."

"Larson, I'm so sorry, are you all right?"

"There's more, Mother, Savannah's pregnant with your grandchild."

Silence.

"Mother, are you there?"

"I'm here son, is my grandchild all right?"

"They're both fighting for their lives. I'm so sorry I had to tell you this way."

"I don't want you to worry about that right now. You have enough on your mind."

Larson couldn't believe what he was hearing, she sounded genuinely concerned.

"I suppose you'll be staying for some time?" said Caroline.

"Yes, Mother, I intend to be here when my baby is born, but I'll keep up with the office; don't worry."

"Larson we can handle the office, just take care of Savannah and the baby." Larson hung up the phone wondering what had just happened. His mother was concerned even caring, not at all like her. He went back into Savannah's room where Maurice and Adele sat watching television.

"My mother sends her prayers for Savannah, and the baby. I told her I would be staying on until they were better. I'll start looking for a hotel in the morning."

"Nonsense," said Adele, "unless the

accommodations we have are not to your liking."

"I would love to stay, I didn't want to impose."

"Larson, you're family now the father of our grandchild. Savannah would want you to stay."

They stayed with Savannah until visiting hours were over then finally left for home.

* * *

Caroline sat at home waiting for Lisette to arrive. She had stopped drinking due to the massive headache she'd had for the last two days.

"Mrs. Mansfield," said Charles, "Ms. Lisette is here to see you."

"Please send her in, Charles, and that will be all."

"Caroline what's wrong? You sounded frantic on the phone."

"Have a seat, Lisette; this could take a while." Caroline told her everything.

"You mean to tell me you ran her off the road?" Lisette shouted.

"I didn't run her off the road, there was a truck coming at her, it crossed the center line. He ran her off the road."

"Dare I ask how she's doing," Lisette asked with a smirk on her face.

Caroline glared at her. "She's in a coma, but that's not the worst part."

"You mean there's something worse?"

"She's pregnant and carrying my grandchild. If

Larson finds out what happen, I will lose them both."

"Does anyone know you were there? I had no idea you were even out of town."

"Larson knows I took a trip. I told him it was for a seminar you talked me into."

"Am I supposed to corroborate your story?"

"If need be, yes. I expect you to, by the way Lisette, where were you? I thought you were going to meet Larson at the hotel."

"I'm so sorry, but my schedule just wouldn't allow it. So where is Larson?" Lisette asked.

"He's in Louisiana with Savannah and the baby."

"Maybe this will all work out, there's a chance she still won't make it."

"What are you saying?" shouted Caroline, "If that happens, I will never forgive myself. I wanted her away from my son, but I never wanted this."

"So you're saying you're okay with them getting together because you feel guilty?"

"I don't know. I just know she's the mother of my grandchild, and like it or not that change's things."

Fifteen

For two months, Savannah and the baby continued to fight for their lives. Adele and Maurice visited the hospital every day. Larson could see the toll it had taken on them. Justine made it as often as her day would allow. Larson found himself living between two countries, flying home only as much as necessary to take care of company business.

He'd come home for the weekend and he and Caroline were out for dinner, so they could talk. They requested a quiet table away from the crowded area. They sat for a while, neither one saying a word. Finally, Caroline asked, "Larson how are Savannah and the baby?"

"They're strong and fighting every day to hang on."

"Larson, I know this is a difficult time, and I don't want to cause you anymore stress, but I have to know."

"Know what?"

"You and Savannah, is it what you really want? Putting everything else aside, if she were healthy would you still want to be with her or is it guilt and sympathy keeping you there."

Larson took his mother's hand in his own. "When she left, I felt as though something was missing in me. When she didn't call, I felt as though my heart had broken. When I thought I would lose her, I felt something die in me. My life without her would be incomplete, whatever the outcome."

Caroline smiled. "I think I'm beginning to understand what she means to you, son."

Larson stared at his mother. "There's something I've been meaning to ask you." She sat up and moved her hands back on the table, ending the rare moment of affection.

"I know this may be difficult for you, Mother, but I want you to come back to Louisiana with me. It would give you an opportunity to see Savannah and meet her parents."

Caroline inhaled deeply. "When are you returning?" she asked Larson.

"I have a flight out Sunday; I booked two seats in case you agreed to go."

"How long will you be staying this time?"

"That will depend on Savannah's condition, but you can return whenever you're ready." He couldn't tell if she was actually considering it, or simply humoring him.

Her expression remained impassive.

"So will you come back with me, Mother?"

"I'll start packing my things in the morning," she said.

Larson couldn't believe it. Maybe his mother would bond with the family, or at the very least accept that he and Savannah would be together. The rest of dinner went perfectly. Larson felt relieved as he spoke of Savannah and their child so freely now that his mother knew about them.

Later, that night Larson called Adele to check on Savannah and the baby.

"Larson, how are you?" she said.

"I'm well, my two babies doing all right?"

"There's been no change with Savannah, but the baby is really growing." Adele told Larson she had a surprise for him and wanted to know whether or not he wanted her to tell him.

"What is it?" he said, anxious to find out.

"We found out the sex of the baby today," she shouted out with such enthusiasm.

Larson heard Maurice in the background yelling, "I thought you were going to wait until he got here."

Larson didn't want to wait. "Tell me, I can't stand it. What are we having?"

"A girl," Adele shouted. You're having a little

girl."

Larson didn't even try to stop the tears rolling down his cheeks.

"I'm having a baby girl." A surge of energy hit him, and before he knew it, he was shouting. He was so excited he almost forgot to tell Adele about his mother coming to visit.

"Adele, I have news as well, my mother has decided to come for a visit."

Adele said nothing.

"Isn't that exciting news?" he asked.

"I am surprised, and it is great news. When should we expect you both?"

"We'll be there Monday morning, and don't worry I'll book a hotel for the two of us."

* * *

Before the plane had even taken off, Caroline had asked for a drink.

"Nerves getting to you, Mother?" asked Larson.

"A little," she said, searching the cabin with her eyes for the stewardess.

"There's nothing to worry about, Mother, her parents are wonderful people."

Caroline sat on the edge of her seat the entire flight.

Once they arrived at the hotel and they'd checked into their room, Larson picked up the phone to call Adele. He let Adele know they'd arrived they were settling in for the night.

"Are you hungry, Mother?" he asked.

"I could eat something, what do you have in mind?"

Larson called for room service. Once the waiter left, Larson took the lids off their meals.

"What is this?" Caroline griped.

"Just try it, it's delicious."

"I'm not terribly hungry, dear; maybe later."

"I'd like to get an early start to the hospital in the morning, Mother, so let's just get some sleep it's been a long night."

The next morning, Larson awoke early as planned, and pushed Caroline to hurry and get ready. "Mother, I need you to be civil to Adele and Maurice. They are good people and they are going through a lot."

"I can behave, Larson. You needn't speak to me like I'm a child."

He knew it would not be easy getting them together. On the way to the hospital Caroline didn't say a word. Instead, she sat staring out the window. If he didn't know better, he would think she was sulking. Larson parked the rental car then opened the door for Caroline.

"We're here, Mother, please remember to be on your best behavior."

Larson tapped on Savannah's door.

"Come in," Adele called. Larson held the door for

his mother while escorting her into the room.

"Adele, Maurice, this is my mother, Caroline. Mother, these are Savannah's parents."

Maurice reached out his hand, giving Adele a little nudge in the small of her back at the same time.

"It is so nice to meet you finally," said Maurice.

"Yes, pleased to meet you," said Adele.

"You as well," said Caroline, "I've heard nothing but good things about you both."

Larson heard Adele whisper softly, "Wish I could say the same."

Larson hid a smile as he hugged them both. With the introductions out of the way, he headed toward Savannah's bed. Caroline turned toward the bed.

"Oh my God," she whispered under her breath. "I'm so sorry for what has happened."

Larson wondered at the peculiar look on his mother's face, but let it go. He wanted to focus on Savannah.

Larson spent the whole time talking to Savannah about the future, as though trying to coerce her back to him.

"It's going to be wonderful, Savannah. The three of us, together, dinner every night, wonderful trips abroad, teaching our baby girl about the wonders of the world." Suddenly, he remembered he had not told Caroline she was going to have a granddaughter.

"Mother, please forgive me, with all the chaos, I

172

failed to mention that Savannah and I are going to have a girl."

"That's wonderful news, son. I'm going to have a granddaughter."

"We're going to have a granddaughter," Adele said abruptly."

"Of course," said Caroline. "We're having a granddaughter."

* * *

The doctor entered the room.

"I'm glad you're all here; there are some things I need to discuss with you."

The room suddenly went quiet with Maurice turning the television off.

"Mr. and Mrs. Monreaux, would you like to discuss this in private?" asked Dr. Vincent.

Adele wanted so badly to get back at Caroline by excluding her from the conversation, only to realize it would hurt Larson, and he didn't deserve any more pain.

"No, we're all family," Adele said before introducing Caroline. "You can speak freely."

"I'm going to need you to consider alternatives if Savannah stays in her current state. The most pressing issue is the baby; she's growing so fast now. The umbilical cord has tightened around her neck. We cannot risk cutting off the oxygen to the brain due to strangulation. That being said, we may have to deliver the baby by C-section which could threaten Savannah's life."

"What are you saying?" Adele shouted. "Are you telling me I may have to choose between my daughter, and my granddaughter?"

"No. There has to be another way," shouted Larson.

"I'm sorry," said Dr. Vincent, "but if she stays in a coma the odds are not in their favor."

Adele ran out of the room crying, she heard Caroline follow behind her. A moment later, she felt Caroline's hand on her shoulder.

"She'll be all right, she's a fighter."

Adele pulled away shouting, "And what do you know about my daughter? She told me how you treated her while in France. You're probably glad this happened, that way you can keep her away from your precious son." Larson and Maurice walked out of the room just in time to catch the end of Adele's ranting.

"Adele," said Maurice, "I thought you weren't going to do this here."

Adele couldn't stop crying, even when Larson put his arm around her.

"It's all right, Adele, you have a right to be angry, just let it out."

He looked at the stunned expression on Caroline's face and had no idea what to say to her. "Adele, why don't you and Maurice get something to eat and a bit of

174

rest?"

Maurice took Adele by the hand. "That's a great idea. I think a break would do us all some good."

Adele looked between the two men and then at Caroline, who had not said a word.

Larson kissed Adele on the cheek. "I'll stay with Savannah and everything will be all right. I don't know how, but I believe it in my heart."

Maurice took Adele by the waist and led her away.

"Mother, are you all right?"

"She's right; everything is my fault, I never meant for this to happen."

"What are you talking about? Of course, this isn't your fault. You had nothing to do with the accident."

Caroline suddenly realized she had said those words aloud.

"Maybe you should get something to eat, Mother. You didn't eat much last night."

"Now you know I don't eat cafeteria food, especially hospital cafeteria food. Do you mind going to get me something edible from outside? I can visit here with Savannah until you get back."

Larson looked at his mother for a moment. "I told Adele I'd stay with Savannah. She wouldn't be happy if she knew I'd left her alone."

"You mean with me, don't you, son. It actually hurts that you don't trust me, when I'm trying my hardest. She's carrying my grand baby; I would never

175

do anything to hurt either of them."

Larson looked at his mother. She really was trying, and he wanted to trust her. "Alright, Mother, you stay with Savannah, and I'll be right back with something for us to eat."

Larson disappeared down the hallway as Caroline entered the room. She stared at Savannah, feeling nothing but remorse. She stood at the doorway, afraid to go in. Finally, she approached the bed, and sat in the chair Larson had sat in earlier.

She reached over taking Savannah's hand in hers, and poured out her heart.

"Savannah If you can hear me right now, I want to say I'm sorry for everything that's happened. You don't know this, but I'm the reason you're here in this hospital bed fighting for your life, and the life of my grand baby. I only meant to follow you. To find out what was going on between you two after I overheard your phone conversation."

She told Savannah everything, hoping it would clear her guilty conscience. "I tried everything to pull the two of you apart, and in all my efforts it has only brought you closer together. If Larson ever finds out what I did, why you're here, I will surely lose my son forever. If I could change anything, it would be what I've done to you. I was unsure of your intentions with my son, but seeing him with you now, I know he loves you." She held Savannah's hand confessing everything to her, as though she were a priest. "I'm sorry," she said, "truly sorry." Suddenly, Caroline felt Savannah's hand squeezing around hers. Caroline jumped, letting go of Savannah's hand as she stood staring by the side of the bed.

"Did she just move? I felt her hand move," Caroline said aloud. Larson walked in the room causing Caroline to scream.

"Mother, what's wrong; you're as white as a ghost?"

Caroline was trembling. "She moved, she moved," Caroline said as she ran toward Larson.

"Mother, please calm down, what are you saying?"

"She moved. Her hand, it moved."

"Calm down, Mother you're imagining things."

"I most certainly am not. I was holding her hand, and she squeezed my hand."

Larson couldn't believe it; he immediately called the nurse into the room and told her what happened.

"I'll get the doctor on the phone; this could be great news," said the nurse. Larson picked up the phone and called Adele, telling her what Caroline told him. Adele was so excited she didn't even question why Caroline was alone in the room with Savannah.

Adele and Maurice arrived at the hospital in record time. "Is it true? Did she move her hand? "Please, tell me exactly what happen?" Adele asked as she turned toward Caroline. "What did she do?"

Caroline took Adele's hand in hers demonstrating what Savannah had done. Adele was so thrilled she grabbed Caroline and hugged her around the neck tight enough to choke her.

"I'm sorry," said Adele, letting go. "I can't believe it. This is fantastic news after all these months."

Savannah's doctors rushed into the room without knocking. "I hear there's been some movement by Savannah," said Dr. Vincent. "Who was here when it happened?"

Caroline spoke up.

"Can you tell me or show me exactly what happened?" asked Dr. Vincent.

"I was holding Savannah's hand and the grip kept getting tighter."

"This is a good sign," the doctor said. "But I don't want you to get your hopes too high. The movement could have been nothing more than the twitching of muscles. If there had been some kind of conversation going on, I might think she was reacting to some type of emotion or sound. Since it appears that is not the case, chances are it was just involuntary movement.

The room went quiet until Adele said, "But there is a chance it was Savannah doing the moving, right?"

"Yes, but a very slight chance, and we still have the issue with the cord around the baby's neck and time is running out." Once the doctors all left the room Adele said, "I know my daughter. She will fight to her

178

last breath. She will not give up."

* * *

Larson convinced Maurice and Adele to go home and get some sleep, and then he went out to talk to Caroline.

"Mother," Larson said, startling her as he touched her on the shoulder. "I'm going to take you back to the hotel to get some rest. I'll come back to stay with Savannah."

"Fine." No argument.

He stepped back into Savannah's room. "I'll be back shortly. I'm going to take my mother back to the hotel. When I get back, you can go and I will stay with Savannah."

The ride was short, as they had booked a hotel close to the hospital. He got his mother settled and ordered some food for her.

"Good night, Mother. I'll see you in the morning."

Larson was sitting on the side of Savannah's bed talking to her when Justine arrived.

"Knock, knock," she said entering the room.

"Larson, I'm sorry I didn't know you were back in town. How are you feeling?"

"Much better," he said. "We've gotten a bit of good news even, though if it comes with a hint of caution,"

"What do you mean?" she asked.

"My mother was holding Savannah's hand earlier

179

today when Savannah squeezed it."

"Are you kidding? That is great news."

They sat talking for hours, both asking many questions of each other. Finally, Justine asked a question that caught him by surprise.

"So, Larson, do you intend to marry Savannah?"

He smiled, never hesitating. "Yes, when she comes through this, I will ask her if she will have me as her husband."

Justine looked at him. "I'll hold you to that you know."

"As her best friend," said Larson, "I would expect nothing less." They both laughed each grabbing hold of Savannah's hands.

* * *

Over the next few weeks, there was no change and they remained concerned about having to take the baby.

Adele had Larson and Caroline over for Sunday dinner. She'd put aside her ill feelings for Caroline the two of them were forging a new friendship. At dinner, everyone spoke of Savannah, Adele had everyone laughing with her stories about Savannah's childhood.

Caroline smiled. "She sounds like a delightfully precocious child."

"I have been blamed for making her into such a tomboy." Maurice tried to hide his smile.

Larson shared his story on how he had bumped

into her in his office. Even Caroline seemed moved by his telling.

"I have to say, I sorely misjudged your daughter. I'm sorry for that."

Adele reached over and patted Caroline's hand and they spent the rest of the evening in relaxed company.

With both Larson and Caroline out of the office for weeks, the time had come for her to return home. She'd booked her flight for that evening. Charles would pick her up at the airport.

Within a week, Larson would return to France as well to take care of some much-needed business. His heart ached every time he left Savannah, and this time would be no different.

Thankfully, Larson wouldn't have to worry about his mother anymore. She and Adele had made peace and were actually getting along.

There still had been no change in Savannah since the day she'd squeezed Caroline's hand. He almost wished his mother would stay, obviously she had said and done something that touched Savannah.

Larson took Caroline to the airport to catch her plane.

"Thank you," he said to her.

"For what, son?"

"For being here when I needed you. I know this wasn't easy for you."

"No," said Caroline, "it wasn't, but I have learned

a lot these last few days."

"Imagine that." Larson gently nudged her and they both laughed.

Sixteen

When Caroline arrived home, she had several messages from Lisette, who sounded a bit out of sorts. She picked up the phone and dialed Lisette's number.

"Mrs. Mansfield, Ms. Lisette is here to see you.

"Lisette, I just got your messages. What is it?"

"I've been calling you for weeks," Lisette all but shrieked. "Where have you been? Why didn't you call me back?"

"Last I checked, I pay my own bills, Lisette, and I answer to no one," Caroline snapped back.

"I didn't mean to insinuate that at all. I was worried."

"I'm fine," Caroline explained. "I've been out of town with my son."

"Business," Lisette asked.

"Not exactly; Larson asked me if I would go and see Savannah with him."

"You went there?" shouted Lisette. "Are you crazy? What if someone had recognized you?"

"Lisette!" Caroline stopped her ranting. "I'm having a grandchild. A little girl; Savannah's pregnant." Caroline was smiling until Lisette said, "How do you know it's Larson's? How do you know it's not a trap, and it's not someone else's child?"

Caroline glared at the hysterical woman. "This is my son's child, and it is my grandchild."

Lisette's face turned a blistering red. "Since when did you decide you're okay with this?" Lisette shouted. "What about me? Where does this leave me? I will not stand for this nonsense, Caroline; you need to fix this."

"Lisette!" Caroline leaned forward. "You were never in love with my son, only his name, and his money. I foolishly went along with it, but no more, it's over. He has found his happiness in someone else; I suggest you let it go, Lisette."

Lisette turned and shouted, "Over? This is far from over. I wonder, what Larson will say when he knows you were in Louisiana the night of Savannah's accident."

Caroline bolted out of her chair. She got in Lisette's face. "Are you threatening me, Lisette?"

"Me? Threatening you?" Lisette laughed, her face twisted into a gruesome expression. "Of course not."

Caroline stood so close to Lisette she could feel her breath on her skin. "You listen, and listen well. If you ever so much as hint a threat to me again, know this, it will be your last. Now, you know where the door is; let yourself out."

Lisette turned, storming out the door.

Caroline would wager that given Lisette's expression, she would heed the warning. What concerned her more was Savannah. She thought about that day at the hospital when Savannah squeezed her hand. What if she heard everything I said? Would she tell Larson if she could? Would they ever allow her near her grandchild? Her head began to pound, so she grabbed some aspirin and decided to take a nap.

* * *

Larson spent the night holding Savannah's hand and hoping she would show some improvement. He feared the doctor might be right about the involuntary movement. The doctors had requested a meeting with all of them to discuss some news. Larson joined Savannah's parents and Justine, who was deemed a part of the family, just as the doctors arrived. "I wanted to show all of you this film in hopes it would better explain why I have come to my decision about Savannah and the baby. It is with a heavy heart I give you this news. We can no longer wait for change in Savannah if the cord is not removed within the next few days, the baby will die."

Adele, who had already been crying for months, immediately burst into tears again.

"Mr. and Mrs. Monreaux, we will do everything in our power to save them both, but there are no guarantees."

Larson asked the doctor, "How many days are we talking?"

"The most we can wait, and still be safe, is three days," said Dr. Vincent. "If any of you have questions, please let me know."

After leaving the room, the family gathered around Savannah. For several minutes they all acted as if nothing were wrong.

Suddenly, Larson jumped up. "We sit here pretending everything is all right, well it's not, and she needs to know that. She needs to know she has to fight. She needs to know she may never see her daughter."

Justine put her hand on his shoulder to calm him. Adele and Maurice stood across from them, shocked by his sudden outburst.

"I'm so sorry," he said. "But she needs to know it's time to fight harder than she's ever fought before."

Justine took him by the hand and led him out into the hallway.

"Larson, I know you're upset, but they have a decision to make that I wouldn't wish on anyone. They may never see their daughter again."

Larson's eyes filled with tears. "What am I going to do without her? How can I raise our daughter without her mother?" Justine put her arms around him.

"We're all here for you, and will be there if you need. Savannah is strong don't you give up on her. Do you hear me? Don't you give up."

Larson pulled himself together and returned to the room. Adele and Maurice stood with their heads bowed in prayer; Larson and Justine joined in.

Maurice called the doctor. "We've all agreed. We want you to proceed with the cesarean section. But we would like two days with our daughter."

No one went home that night. Everyone took shifts, staying in the room and praying in the chapel.

Larson called Caroline to tell her the news.

"I'm so sorry, son. Are you all right?"

He tried to keep the pain out of his voice. "I will keep you abreast of everything, Mother, try not to worry."

"You have no idea how sorry I am, Larson."

Dr. Vincent stopped in during his rounds the next morning. "We've schedule the procedure for tomorrow morning at 10:00 o'clock. I'd like you all to go home and get some rest."

"Everyone else should go," Adele insisted. "I'll be staying with my daughter."

"Oh no," said Dr. Vincent, "I don't think that is a good idea. I need you rested for tomorrow; Savannah will need you as well."

Larson spoke up. "I'll stay if it's all right, that way everyone else can go home and get some rest."

Maurice convinced Adele and Justine it was for the best. There had been co-workers and friends visiting all day, and it was late.

"Larson, please take care of my little girl tonight. We will see you in the morning," said Adele.

Larson hadn't eaten since lunch, but his stomach had been upset for days. He turned on the television and flipped through the channels several times, only to turn it off again. He'd brought a book with him, the same one he'd read pages from to Savannah while she was in France. He opened it, and began to read to himself at first, then aloud to Savannah.

He read nonstop until 3:00 in the morning when his eyes burned so badly he couldn't focus anymore. He took Savannah by the hand saying, "I know with all my heart you can hear me. I need you to listen, and understand what I'm going to tell you. Our little girl's umbilical cord is wrapped around her neck, and starting to stop the flow of oxygen to her brain."

He spoke as though she was looking at him, he told her everything the doctor had said, right down to the possibility that she might not make it. "I cannot do this without you," he said. "I need you to help me raise our little girl." He held her hand against his cheek, allowing his tears to roll down her fingers. "You are the strongest person I know. Fight, Savannah; hear my voice and please come back to me."

He trembled as he squeezed her hand. He'd

gripped it so tight he barely noticed when it moved. He had his head down when he thought he heard a small whimper. He raised his head and found himself looking into Savannah's eyes.

Tears rolled down the side of her face. He shouted for the nurse, pressing the call button over and over. "Come quick! Her eyes are open."

A team of doctors and nurses flooded the room. They checked her pupils and she actually responded.

"Savannah can you try to speak?" the doctor asked. She moved her mouth, but nothing came out. "Get Dr. Vincent and his team on the phone, stat."

Larson didn't want to alarm Adele, but knew he had to call and tell them the news. The phone rang; Adele picked it up before the first ring ended.

"Hello."

"Adele, this is Larson." Before he could get another word out, she burst into hysterical tears.

"Adele, calm down please, its good news."

"What did you say?" she asked.

"I have good news, Savannah's eyes are open. I heard her trying to speak."

Adele shook Maurice telling him to get dressed, they had to get to the hospital. She would explain everything on the way. Justine had stayed the night at their house and was already awake.

"Get dressed, Justine, were going to the hospital. She's awake."

Larson listened as the family rushed around. She hadn't even hung up the phone before rushing out the door.

When they arrived at the hospital, the room was swarming with doctors and nurses. Larson met Adele at the door.

"Larson, where is she?"

"It's all right, Adele. Their running test on her right now, it shouldn't be much longer."

"What happened? What did she say to you?"

"I told her everything. I told her she might not make it, and that I needed her to fight–for me and the baby."

Adele frowned, her disapproval obvious, but she held her tongue.

"While pleading with Savannah, I thought I heard a mutter or a whisper. When I looked up, her eyes were open and tears were rolling down her face."

Adele grabbed a hold of Maurice. "I need to sit down."

After what seemed like the longest two hours ever, the doctors returned to the room with Savannah.

Adele grabbed her hand saying, "Savannah can you hear me?"

"She nodded her head slowly."

The doctors asked everyone to leave the room except for family.

"I'm glad you're all here, we are witness to a

remarkable event. The mere fact she survived the accident is a miracle in itself, but to have her suddenly awaken is truly astonishing. I'm going to tell you everything we know, and don't know.

"We know there is no brain damage or neurological damage."

"Why can't she speak?" Larson could barely stand still.

"We don't know, but we think it's just a matter of time before she does. She has a long road of therapy ahead, but in time she should return to a normal life. As you all know, we were scheduled for surgery today to remove the baby. Under the circumstances, we now have other options."

"What options?" Maurice asked, jumping up.

"With her conscious now, we would be able to un-wrap the cord while delivery is in progress provided it doesn't cause any distress to the baby. My concern is we would have to induce labor, and she would be under an enormous amount of stress. Honestly, I'm not sure she's ready for that kind of trauma. I suggest we give her one more day, and see how she's doing tomorrow."

"Thank you, Dr. Vincent, you've definitely given us plenty to think about," said Maurice.

Before the door could close, everyone had gathered around the bed talking, laughing, and crying. They had truly received a miracle, and their prayers had been answered. They spent the day hugging her, and telling her what had been going on since the accident. She tried to speak. Her lips moved, but she still made no sounds.

Larson stroked her forehead. "Don't try so hard to speak it will come in time."

Savannah blinked her eyes in an attempt to communicate.

They all spent the rest of the day. It appeared that no one wanted to go home. Finally, the nurse put her foot down.

"You all need to go. It's late and she needs to rest."

"I'll be staying."

Everyone tried to argue, but Larson refused to leave. "Don't worry; I'll call if there is anything new to report."

He suddenly remembered that he had not told his mother the positive news. He leaned over and kissed Savannah on her forehead. She looked at him, her eyes imploring, and touched her lips.

"Are you sure? I don't want to hurt you."

Savannah laughed, though no one could hear it, as she touched her lips again. Larson leaned in and kissed her. She held his face in her hands, and he began to cry. She kissed the tears as they rolled down his face. "It's all right," she mouthed. "Go ahead."

"You know, she came to see you."

He laughed when Savannah scowled.

"She is different. I'm not sure how, or why, but she isn't the same person."

She waved him toward the door.

"I'll be right outside, sweetheart. I promise I won't be long."

Savannah smiled; she remembered those green eyes from the coffee house. It seemed so long ago. From what they'd told her, she'd lost so much time while in a coma. Could she ever make up that time?

When Larson walked out to call Caroline, it was the first time Savannah had been alone since coming out of the coma. Her stomach quivered and she moved her hand toward her stomach, feeling a slight discomfort.

When she felt the size of her stomach, she realized they had not told her everything. It was almost as if she had forgotten she were pregnant.

She began to cry, slowly rubbing her hand back and forth across her now large belly. My baby she thought, how is my baby? Panic surged through her and she tried to call out to Larson, but no sounds came out. Frantic, she began knocking things off the table praying he would hear her.

He rushed into the room. Savannah was sitting up crying holding her belly.

"Savannah what's wrong? Are you hurting?"

She shook her head, pointing at her stomach.

"Are you asking about the baby?"

She nodded, scared of what had happened.

"The baby's fine, we have a beautiful baby girl who can't wait for you to be her mother."

Savannah felt herself calming as she stared down at her stomach and she gently rubbed it.

Larson grabbed a pencil and paper for Savannah so she could write anything she might want to say.

He told her how much he loved her, and he couldn't envision life without her.

She told him she'd dreamed about him, or at least she thought it was a beautiful dream.

They continued to talk, with Savannah writing notes, and Larson answering, until she finally fell asleep holding his hand.

* * *

Caroline wasn't sure how much more she could take. Her stress level had risen. With Savannah awake, it could be just a matter of time. Even though she could not speak now, that could change at any minute.

She was genuinely happy Savannah was doing so well, but she knew it could mean the end of her family. It would be painful enough if she took her son away, but to take the only grandchild she may ever have would be unbearable.

She poured herself a drink. "You have no one to blame but yourself," she said aloud. "Now I'll have to face the consequences."

Seventeen

When everyone arrived at the hospital, Larson let them know Savannah was not allowed anything to eat or drink until they decided how to proceed

The doctor joined them with a smile. "We will be inducing labor today. It's time we get this baby born."

He went on to explain that it could still take hours before Savannah might be ready to deliver.

With everyone else chattering and speculating, Larson went out to the lobby to call Caroline and relay the news.

"Hello," she answered on the first ring.

"Mother, are you waiting on a phone call?"

"Son, hello, how are things going with Savannah?"

"That's why I've called, Mother. The doctors will be inducing labor, and I was hoping you might be able to get here for the birth of your grandchild, or at least shortly after."

Larson waited for his mother's response. Was she back to her old self? Had she tired of being kind?

"Mother, are you there?"

"Yes, I'm here. I'll get a flight out as soon as possible."

"That's wonderful, Mother. I'll let Savannah know you're on your way."

"No, don't tell her; I want it to be a surprise."

She almost sounded desperate, but he pushed it off as anxious. "Alright, Mother. I won't tell her, but keep me posted on your flight, and I can pick you up at the airport."

After disconnecting the call, Larson went back to Savannah's room. She was sitting up. One of her legs still in a cast and she had faint signs of bruising on her body.

Savannah began waving her hand at Adele.

"What is it, dear?"

Savannah scribbled on the notebook Larson had gotten her.

How will they do this with my leg the way it is?

"Don't worry baby, I'm sure they've got everything under control," said Adele.

Justine and Savannah had been talking about the baby and how they couldn't wait to see her.

Before long the doctor came back in. "It's time to head over to the birthing room. We'll be monitoring you during the birth process."

Everyone stood and the doctor laughed. "Only one of you can be in the room with her. I will leave it up to you all to decide amongst yourself."

Adele stepped over to Larson. "You should be there for the birth of your daughter. We were there for ours, and there's nothing like it in the world."

Larson pulled Adele into an embrace.

"I promise I'll take good care of her."

"I know you will, Larson."

Larson wandered in and out of the birthing room. The lobby had once again filled with friends and coworkers sitting around, talking. Larson and the doctor took turns going out every so often to report on how things were going.

Larson thought he was holding up well until Savannah wrote him a note telling him to stop pacing and sit still because he was making her nervous.

Eight hours in, the labor began, but it could still be hours before she delivered. They'd modified the room with her injuries in mind, incorporating a vast array of special devices to aid her during delivery.

* * *

By the time Savannah began the actual birthing with Larson holding her hand and offering support, the waiting room had emptied except for Adele, Maurice, and Justine.

"Savannah," said Dr. Martin, the cord has been removed from around the baby's neck, and now I need

197

you to push."

"You can do this, sweetheart." Larson squeezed her hand and smiled down at her.

Savannah pushed. She gasped for air and pushed. After fifteen minutes of pushing, she fell back, exhausted.

"That's my girl," Larson crooned.

She glared up at him as Dr. Martin instructed her to push again. Savannah did.

"Okay, Savannah, I need you to give me one big push."

Savannah, bore down with all her might, and tried to push. All at once, two voices filled the room. First came the cries of their beautiful baby girl, then the sound of Savannah's voice. She had somehow found her voice.

Larson looked down at her. "Was that you? Did you just scream?"

The doctor handed her the baby. "Today we have miracles, two for one."

Savannah cried and laughed and cried again when she looked up at Larson staring down at them. She turned her attention back to their beautiful daughter with her father's hair and eyes and her mother's skin tone.

Dr. Martin congratulated them both. "I'll go and tell your family the news. The rest of the team will see to all your needs. I be back in a bit."

* * *

Caroline's flight had made it in, but she was unable to reach Larson on the phone, so she called a taxi to take her to the hospital. She arrived in time to see the doctor walking away. Chatter and laughter echoed through the waiting room as she walked up.

She made her way through the crowd and found Adele and Maurice. "Adele, what's going on?"

"They're okay. They're both okay," shouted Adele as she hugged Caroline around the neck.

"What do you mean they're okay?"

Savannah is conscious and talking, and the baby is beautiful and well."

"Oh thank God," said Caroline. She was so relieved, but abruptly remembered what she had told Savannah about the accident. Her heart raced, but she forced herself not to look concerned.

Larson practically stumbled into the lobby; Caroline could tell her son hadn't had much sleep over the last few days.

He grabbed Adele and Maurice. "She's fine, they're both fine."

Caroline tapped him on the shoulder.

"Mother, you made it. When did you get here?" He pulled her into a hug and after a few awkward moments, she hugged him back.

"Just recently. I am so proud of you, Larson."

"Mother, is that a tear in your eye I see?"

199

Caroline brushed it away; she'd never shown such emotion in front of others before.

She stood by as Larson addressed the jubilant crowd.

"I want to thank each and every one of you for all the love and support you've shown. You will always have my undying gratitude. Savannah and I will never forget this."

Caroline watched the crowd gather in and embrace her son. The warmth and love radiating in the room felt almost foreign to her. She stood back until the crown simmered down and started to disperse.

"I know you want to be with Savannah, but I think you should go back to your room and get cleaned up. You don't look so good."

"That's a good idea, Mother. I want to make a good impression on my daughter."

* * *

Adele and Maurice waited with Justine in Savannah's room. They would be bringing her in any time.

Adele clasped her hands over her heart as the nurse brought Savannah into the room. Tears filled everyone's eyes when Savannah spoke.

"Hello."

They gathered around her, kissing and hugging her. Adele, who had been crying for months, couldn't find any more tears.

"I'm so happy to see you," Adele said. "I've missed you so much, Savannah." She put her hands on her daughter's face. "You're a mother now and there's no other feeling like it in the world, is there?"

Savannah gazed around the room looking for Larson.

Adele noticed. "He'll be back. He took Caroline to the hotel."

"Caroline's here?" Savannah asked, her voice hoarse and raspy.

"Yes," said Adele, "she is so happy you're all right. She can't wait to see our grandchild."

Dr. Martin stepped into the room. "I'm going to ask you all to go home for the night. Savannah has been through quite a trauma and she needs to rest–alone."

"But Larson hasn't gotten back," Adele argued.

"He can go to the nursery and see the baby, but I want this room empty except for our little miracle, here." Dr. Martin patted Savannah's hand.

"Mama, can you let Larson know? Tell him I'll be waiting for him in the morning."

"Of course, dear. We'll go see the baby before we go. You call me if you need anything. Anything at all." Adele turned and challenged Dr. Martin to say anything.

* * *

Savannah lay with her eyes wide open for a while

trying to sleep, but she had too much on her mind, the most confusing, what to say to Caroline. She couldn't help but wonder what would become of her, and Larson now that they were parents.

The door opened, startling her. The nurse handed her the baby.

"So have you chosen a name yet?"

Savannah looked up. "Oh my, in all the confusion I haven't even given it a moment's thought."

She sat there gazing at her beautiful daughter. "You look so much like your dad, little one," she said while playing with her fingers. "So what do we name you? What about Rose or Olive? I've got it. What about Iris? Oh let's face it, I don't have a clue what to name you. We'll just leave it up to daddy."

Savannah hummed softly as she nursed her daughter. "You certainly are a miracle."

A short time later, the nurse came in to get the baby. "Can I get you anything to sleep?"

"No, thank you, I think I can manage on my own." Savannah pulled the covers over her arms and closed her eyes.

Savannah awoke to the sounds of people shushing and trying to whisper. Maurice and Adele had slipped into the room and were preening like peacocks.

"She's a beautiful baby, isn't she."

"She sure is, Adele." Her father puffed out his chest, as proud as any grandpa could be.

"Spoiling her already, you two?" said a voice from behind as they all turned to discover Justine standing there.

"Good morning!" They spoke at the same time.

"I won't be able to stay long I'm on my way into work. I wanted to see Savannah, and the baby before going in."

Adele hugged Justine. "Did you go to the nursery?"

"You bet, they said you two had just come up here."

"Good morning to you all too," Savannah finally said. She was sitting up eating her breakfast.

They all laughed. "How was your night, sweetheart?" Maurice moved first and kissed her on the forehead.

"Restful," she said. She'd spent quite some time considering the months of therapy ahead of her. Her leg ached inside her cast and she still hated seeing the bruises on most parts of her body.

A tap on the door had them all turning back toward the door. Larson walked in with flowers in hand, and Caroline trailing behind him.

"Good morning," he said to everyone as he made his way to Savannah, kissing her on the forehead.

Caroline peeked from behind. "Good morning, Savannah; how are you feeling?"

"Much better than a few months, ago Caroline,

thank you for asking."

Caroline sat in the corner, and Savannah could have sworn she was trying hard not to be seen.

"Larson, have you seen your little girl this morning?" Savannah asked in an effort to get Caroline alone.

"Not since last night. I came right up. Mother, would you like to go with me to the nursery and see your granddaughter?"

Caroline rose in a hurry to follow Larson

"If it's okay with everyone, I'd like to speak with Caroline alone for a moment," Savannah managed to get out.

Her parents looked at each obviously wondering what Savannah wanted to say to Caroline. They knew Caroline and Savannah had had many differences over the past months.

Justine mouthed, "I'll be right outside the door." She held up both her fists and Savannah laughed.

Larson took Savannah's hand and asked her if she wanted him to stay. "I'm fine; would you all just go." She pulled him down and kissed him.

The room went quiet, but everyone filed out.

"Caroline," Savannah said, "come out of the corner so I can see you. We need to talk."

Caroline got up and walked around the bed, sitting in the chair next to Savannah. Before Savannah could say anything Caroline began speaking. "I know I'm the last person you want to see right now, and you have every right if you want to keep me away from my grandchild. I'm not the same person you met in France those many months ago."

Before she could say anything more, Savannah stopped her. "Caroline, the reason I wanted to speak with you alone is because I wanted to tell you I did hear you that day. At first, I thought it was a dream, but it was so vivid it brought me back to that very night. I realized you had to have been the one following me."

Caroline went to speak, but again Savannah stopped her.

"Just listen, Caroline, let me finish." As Savannah continued on, she reminded Caroline of all the reasons she should tell Larson what happen.

Caroline interrupted. "So you will take my son, and grandchild away from me. It would be no more than I deserve."

Savannah took Caroline by the hand, looked into her eyes and said, "I love your son, with all my heart, and hurting him to get back at you will not make me feel better. I have a child, your grandchild. It wouldn't be right for me to tear his family apart for revenge. I heard you that night, every word, I know with all my heart, you didn't mean for this to happen." She put her hand on Caroline's cheek, looked her in the eyes, and said, "We're a family now, and from this day forward we never speak of this again. No one needs to know."

Caroline grabbed Savannah around the neck and hugged her. "My son was right to fall in love with you. You have a beauty that goes far beyond just the physical."

"So are you ready to meet your granddaughter?"

"More than anything," said Caroline.

Savannah told her to call everyone back in the room, and she would get the nurse to bring in the baby.

When Caroline stepped out her face glowed. Savannah stifled a giggle as Larson, Adele, Maurice, and Justine all stared, as if waiting for something to happen.

Savannah pressed her call button. When the nurse came in, Savannah asked her to bring in the baby.

Everyone waited, anxious to see the baby up close for the first time. While they waited they all yelled out baby names. While watching her family argue, warmth wrapped around Savannah–her grandmother.

"Iris Odette." Everyone turned toward her.

"Savannah, honey, are you sure?" said Adele.

She turned to Larson, saying, "If it's all right with her father?"

"Her father loves the name," he said, but there's one thing missing." He knelt next to Savannah, took out a ring, and said, "Savannah Monreaux, will you marry me?"

Tears rolled down her cheeks. "Oh, yes. I'll marry

you."

There wasn't a dry eye in the room when Savannah accepted the ring.

Larson held up the baby. "I would like to present to you, our daughter, Iris Odette Mansfield."

Adele smiled at Savannah "Your grandmother would be so proud you've given Iris her middle name."

In that moment, Savannah realized she'd always been waiting, waiting for love, waiting for a family of her own, waiting to be accepted. The time had come, she was no longer Savannah in waiting.

Felicia Gaines lives in South Texas with her husband and their wonderful dog, D'artanian. She is a native of Louisiana and moved to Texas several years ago.

She is a 2003 graduate of Louisiana State University in Baton Rouge with a B.S. in psychology. She has spent the last twenty-three years, however, in the engineering field from which she has retired.

In 2005, her life changed dramatically after several heart attacks and two open heart surgeries. She is now pursuing her first love of writing and enjoying every minute of it.

http://FeliciaGaines.wordpress.com

https://www.facebook.com/felicia.gainesmartin